A Prize for All Saints

Don Santina

BookLocker

St. Petersburg, Florida

Published by BookLocker.com, Inc., St. Petersburg, Florida.

Printed on acid-free paper.

This book is a work of fiction. Names, characters, places and incidents either are the product of the author's imagination or are used fictitiously. Any resemblance to actual events, persons, or locales, living or dead, is entirely coincidental.

BookLocker.com, Inc.
2020

Library of Congress Cataloguing in Publication Data
Santina, Don
A Prize for All Saints by Don Santina
Library of Congress Control Number: 2020921670

For Laura, Peter, Lin, Dante and Dominic . . . and for
Grandpa Humphrey who sang the songs
and told the stories.

PROLOGUE

San Francisco, California, December, 1929

It was late afternoon and the first drops of rain were falling as the young nun hurried down Howard Street to the convent. Her face flushed bright red, she slipped her copy of the San Francisco *Call-Bulletin* newspaper inside her black habit and bounded up the stairs to the convent door. She paused a moment to regain her composure and then rang the bell. Almost immediately a small black grid near the top of the heavy door slid back.

"*Quis tu es?*" an unseen voice asked.

"Sister Agatha."

"*Intro.*"

The door swung open silently. Sister Agatha murmured "*Deo Gratias*" toward the dark presence behind the door and walked respectfully down the Lysol-scented hallway to the staircase at the end. Upon turning the corner, she took the stairs two at a time and was soon in her cubicle on the second floor. The room was just big enough for a single bed and a desk with a chair. There was a small closet with three shelves and three hangers for clothing, and there was a simple brown crucifix on the white plastered wall above the bed. The linoleum-covered floor was bare; the room was cold.

Sister Agatha sat down in the chair, flicked on the single-bulb lamp and spread the newspaper on the desk, quickly finding the page she wanted in the second section. She held her breath.

"Missing Link Found in China!" announced the bold-faced headline on the top of page fourteen. She withdrew rimless spectacles from her left sleeve and leaned into the newspaper. In her intensity, she did not realize that her lips were moving as she read, a fault she had spent years trying to correct.

Peking, China – Scientists from the Peking Union Medical College announced on Tuesday that they have unearthed a skull which they claim is the oldest form of the human species discovered to date. A team led by a Canadian anthropologist, Davidson Black, found the nearly intact skullcap in a deep chasm of fossilized clay in nearby Choukoutien where teams have been digging for over a decade. Fossilized human teeth have been found at the site during the past three years. Black has named the discovery Simanthropus Pekinensis or "Peking Man." "Peking Man was a thinking being, standing erect, dating to the beginning of the Ice Age," Black claimed.

Professor Herman Franck of the Department of Anthropology at the University of California stated that "it appears that Black and his team of Chinese anthropologists has found the first human-like creature that is not an ape. For people who accept Darwin's theory of evolution, the 'Peking Man' could be the 'missing link' between the ape and modern man."

The nun closed her eyes, took a deep breath and slowly exhaled. Then she returned to the article.

Black's work is sponsored by the Peking Union Medical College where he previously taught anatomy. After the fossilized teeth were found three years ago, Black persuaded the Rockefeller Foundation to financially support a large scale excavation at the site. The actual discovery of the skull was made by W.C. Pei, a Chinese paleontologist. The fossils are being examined, tested and stored at the College. It should be noted here that the Darwinian Theory has not been completely accepted by all authorities. Four years ago, John Scopes, a teacher in Tennessee, was convicted and fined for teaching Darwinian evolution in his high school classroom.

Sister Agatha read the article twice and then carefully cut it out with a cuticle scissors. She folded it several times and squeezed it inside the leather cover of her hymnal. The newspaper she would dispose of later.

ONE

Leyte, the Philippines, December 1944

"Baker Two, Baker Two! This is Baker One! Japanese everywhere! We are being overrun! Hold your position! Hold your position! Do you read me?"

The walkie talkie crackled and was silent. Lieutenant John Maletesta looked at Corporal James "Lonnie" Vennemeyer. They could hear the small arms fire increasing on their right flank about a mile away. Maletesta pushed the walkie talkie button down.

"Baker One, this is Baker Two. Do you read? Come in, Baker One. Over."

There was no answer.

"Baker One, come in. Come in, Baker One," Maletesta repeated.

"Looks like Captain Calloway's in for it," Vennemeyer said. Vennemeyer had a long-jawed face with naturally doleful eyes. He peered out into the encroaching darkness as if he could see Calloway's unit.

"And nothing we can do about it. Damn!" He took a deep breath and slowly exhaled. "Lonnie, pull the scouts in and gather up the rest. We'll dig in here on the high ground."

"Yes sir."

Vennemeyer disappeared silently into the trees. Maletesta scanned his "high ground": a slight rise in the forest floor dotted with small boulders and clumps of brush. From here, Maletesta's platoon could form a 360 degree perimeter to defend themselves. The scene from Hemingway's "Fight on the Hilltop" flitted through his mind as he reviewed the position, but he brushed it away quickly.

I'm not El Sordo, and there's no air force to worry about here.

Maletesta removed his helmet and scratched his head, contemplating the position around him. He had black curly hair and a hawky nose which separated hazel eyes that were called enchanting by his girlfriend and scary by an opposing pitcher. He strode around the site with an athlete's grace, calculating fields of fire.

A few minutes later, the platoon emerged from the trees and gathered quietly around him. Counting the two Filipino scouts, there were only fourteen of them left. They had slept in the rain the night before and had kept moving all day. They were hot and tired and shifted on their feet as they stood in formation. In the six weeks since the landing, they had been in at least one firefight with the enemy every other day. Maletesta quietly pointed out a position to each man as he circled the hill with them. They pulled out their shovels and began digging in as the small arms fire diminished and the sky grew dark. They ate cold rations and waited. There was little talking between them. Fortunately, there was a full moon, so there would be no surprise attack.

At eight o'clock by Maletesta's watch, the gunfire at Baker One's position ceased. The night was quiet with the exception of a pair of eagle-owls calling to each other and a slight high breeze rustling the leaves.

"Captain Calloway?" whispered Vennemeyer, who came up on Maletesta's left.

"Maybe some of them made it back to the river. Anyway, be ready. *Pazienza*, huh?" Maletesta replied.

"Yeah, yeah, I know--patience. Between you and Barreras, lieutenant, by the time this war is over, I'll know three languages." Vennemeyer returned to his position.

Maletesta whistled low in imitation of a night bird. One by one, each man in the platoon answered. They were in place and ready. Maletesta checked the chamber of his M1 carbine.

Satisfied that there was a cartridge in it, he pushed the safety off and peered down the slope.

Nothing.

He settled his legs farther into the shallow depression he had dug behind the rocks. He brushed some dirt off the walnut stock of the carbine and his thoughts went inexplicitly to his mother's walnut dining room table. He could smell the red oil he used to polish the table on the holidays. He thought of Annemarie and their Christmas Eve date and smiled.

Maybe they're not coming this way.

Maletesta set the carbine down, reached into his pack and pulled out a battered baseball.

His good luck charm, the home run ball he hit during the tryout at Seals Stadium. He squeezed it and tossed it in the air catching it lightly.

I'll be back.

He squeezed the ball hard.

I'll be back.

Abruptly, he shoved the ball back down into the pack and picked up the carbine.

Have I forgotten anything?

He had placed the .30 machine gun facing the densest part of the woods. The rest were in a rough circle about 60 feet in diameter with the two grease guns on opposite sides. Lonnie with his BAR was in the center, in reserve, ready to back up any weak spot.

Wait a minute! Something moved. That bush wasn't there before.

Maletesta squeezed off a shot into a bush about fifty yards down the slope. The bush jumped and yelled and he fired two more rounds into it.

"Banzai! Banzai! Banzai!"

All hell broke loose on all sides. The bottom of the slope around the perimeter was alive with crawling, running, and dodging Japanese soldiers. Maletesta emptied his carbine, shoved another banana clip in, and emptied that one too. He was aware of the intense gunfire around him, the furious bursts from the full automatics and the steady blasts of the Ml's. Bullets from the enemy fire buzzed around him, smacking into trees and rocks.

He looked back quickly at Lonnie and over at Jimmie Higgins on his right. Higgins' M1 had jammed and he was trying desperately to clear it.

"Lonnie, cover Jimmie!" Maletesta yelled.

Vennemeyer slid in behind Higgins, firing as he moved.

"Jesus! I'm hit! I'm hit! Oh, Jesus, I'm hit!"

It was Daly, about twenty feet from Maletesta's left. He had dropped his rifle and rolled out from behind his tree, clutching his side. Maletesta could see three Japanese soldiers moving quickly up the slope toward Daly. He stood up and ran to Daly, firing rapidly at the three shapes on the slope. One of them fell; the other two fired back at Maletesta and then retreated back down the slope. He pulled Daly back behind the tree, just as a Japanese non-com suddenly appeared out of nowhere, a Nambu pistol in one hand and a samurai sword in the other. As he saw Maletesta, they both fired simultaneously. The non-com's shot went wild. Maletesta's hit its mark and the non-com sank to the ground.

As suddenly as the engagement began, it was over. The firing stopped. The air was heavy with the smell of gunpowder and the groans of the wounded and dying. Maletesta's platoon could hear the Japanese crashing back through the woods in full flight. They reloaded their weapons and watched the forest warily.

Maletesta tore Daly's shirt open and looked at the nasty oozing hole below his rib cage. Daly's face was pale, and he writhed in pain.

"You'll be alright, Mike, you're going home," Maletesta said and motioned to Higgins, who carried the medical bag, to bring the morphine. "You'll be back with Millie before you know it, Mike. You're a lucky guy. Hurry up, Jimmie. That's it."

Felipe Barreras, one of the scouts, scooted over to where Maletesta sat, taking stock of the situation.

A miracle, only one wounded.

"I see if they're really gone?" whispered Barreras.

"OK, *kaibigan*. Careful though. So far, so good," Maletesta smiled and punched

Barreras on the shoulder. Barreras gave a thumbs-up back to Maletesta.

Barreras slipped down the slope and Maletesta watched him disappear into the forest.

Then he stood up cautiously and stepped out from behind the tree. The non-com was sprawled over its roots. There was no movement in the woods.

They're gone, thank God.

He leaned the carbine against the tree and lit a cigarette. He exhaled loudly and shook his head in disbelief at Vennemeyer, who stood at a nearby tree, scanning the forest. Only one wounded. Vennemeyer held the BAR loosely at his side.

"Luck o' the Irish, Lonn…"

Suddenly, the Japanese non-com was on his feet, swinging his sword. Instinctively, Maletesta raised his left arm in defense and tried to back step. In a blur he saw the flash of the blade slicing through his arm and the blood spurting out. He screamed. He saw the non-com hammered back by a burst from Lonnie's BAR. He saw his arm on the ground. He screamed again. And again.

TWO

Burlingame, California, 1946

"Success in this venture is inevitable, Sister. I don't think it would be presumptuous of me to say 'Eureka!'"

Professor Hombardt paused and smiled smugly. He picked up a wooden pointer and continued his presentation.

Sister Agatha Buckley, president of the College of All Saints, removed her rimless bifocals and polished them with the white handkerchief she kept in her sleeve as Hombardt's precise voice marched onward, laying fact upon fact to an electrifying conclusion. *Success.* Her fingers rubbed vigorously and efficiently around each lens as she inhaled deeply. *Acclaim.* Then she exhaled on the glass and gave a final rub. *Credibility.*

The College of All Saints is located in the small suburban town of Burlingame, California, about twenty miles south of San Francisco. The stucco buildings form a quadrant nestled in the low hills at the foot of the Coast Range. Their Spanish tile roofs give one the impression of a mission colony. Morning fog disappears at about noon and the temperature can rise to the high seventies by three o'clock. Birds call to each other throughout the day as the old men who serve as groundskeepers push lawn mowers and trim shrubs. Neighboring cattle frequently stare over the fences at the six hundred and seventeen young female students scurrying to their classes.

This was a Friday afternoon in the spring of 1946. A presentation was ending in the sticky warmth of an Anthropology classroom in the modest one-story building called the Hall of Science. The near empty classroom had a high ceiling with three long sectional windows along one wall. Shades were pulled over the windows in a not very successful effort to darken the room. At a desk in the rear of the room, a student sat with her hand poised over the mechanism of a slide projector mounted on an adjoining desk. Her eyes were concentrated on the figure standing in the front of the classroom, waiting anxiously for her cue to change slides.

The image projected on the front wall was that of a prehistoric human jawbone. A rubber-tipped pointer indicated an area near the mandible. At the other end of the pointer stood Professor Richard Rossi Hombardt, Ph.D., Anthropology, 1919, University of Chicago.

"The next slide, please, Miss Wilson."

Hombardt's diction was as crisp as befitted his physical persona: ramrod straight, his hair trimmed to accentuate his graying temples and meticulously attired in a poplin three button suit.

The mechanism clanked and on the wall there appeared a grainy photograph of a cave entrance in a mountainside. The image hung momentarily in the air and was then followed by a colored map of the island of Borneo. Hombardt tapped the center of the island triumphantly and then turned to the two people sitting in the front row of the semi-darkness.

"And so you see, Sister Agatha," Hombardt's straight white teeth shone in the reflected light of the projector, "the case is indeed very strong for the origin of what we know as *homo sapiens* to be in Borneo. The ancestor of mankind…here!"

He jabbed at the map with his pointer.

"The evidence is overwhelming. Just think of it, Sister Agatha! Neanderthal Man, Java Man, Peking Man, and now…Borneo Man," he paused, "discovered by the College of All Saints!"

Hombardt brought his arm down and held the pointer in both hands in a mock present-arms position. His voice quivered, "History awaits us."

C. Allen Willis, his assistant professor, almost applauded but restrained himself to a vigorous nut-cracker nodding at the silent nun next to him.

"Congratulations, Doctor Hombardt," Sister Agatha said slowly, "this is indeed a full and fragrant dream." She replaced her eyeglasses on the middle of her nose and changed gears.

"However, even if I accept your conclusion and also recognize that such a discovery would be a tremendous boon to our humble college, how could we carry out such an expedition? Our entire anthropology department consists of you and Mister Willis here and some undergraduates. I don't believe that any of you have had very much experience in the field."

The nun pulled herself out of the desk and gestured to the student to raise the shades. She grimaced slightly as she straightened her back. She was a round, slightly arthritic woman of forty-seven and the student desk did not suit her for any length of time. As she stood, she smoothed out creases in her black habit.

"Ah, now there's where you're mistaken, Sister," said Hombardt, "I've been on digs in Palestine, Montana, and Arizona. As you know, I was a supply officer in Washington during the war. There will be no problem in organizing this expedition."

Hombardt tugged arrogantly at his tie.

"As a matter of fact, I've already begun preparations."

"Pardon me?"

"I've arranged for a highly-recommended guide in Sibu, Sarawak, to lead us to the caves."

"Doctor Hombardt! You've had no authorization!" Sister Agatha's bright blue eyes were livid.

"And I've been on many overnights on Mount Tamalpais," Willis chipped in, nervously.

He was quite pleased with the progress of things and had remained in his desk jotting down notes in his journal.

"Shut up, Willis," Hombardt snapped. "Sister, surely you know how important…"

"That's enough, Doctor Hombardt."

Sister Agatha had taken the chair at the teacher's desk. She looked steadily at Hombardt, who stood defiantly, arms across his chest, chin pointed at some imaginary target on the wall behind the nun.

"I'm well aware of your experience and your scholarship, Doctor Hombardt. And yours, Mister Willis."

Her words were spoken in well measured tones.

"However," she continued, "an expedition in the wilds of Borneo is an entirely different and dangerous situation. According to the *National Geographic* magazines in our library, tribes still war with each other in the interior. If that weren't enough, there's the jungle--bugs, snakes, quicksand, river pirates, and heaven's above, volcanoes and earthquakes!

"Earthquakes, mind you!" Sister Agatha shuddered. "Gentlemen, I have vivid memories of our 1906 quake. It was not exactly the picnic in the park that is depicted in the tourist brochures."

Hombardt shifted slightly on his feet, but his face remained still.

"Getting back to Borneo," she said slowly, emphasizing each word, "there are also no roads in the interior. It goes without saying that this is a very dangerous place. Neither of you have had experience in these kinds of circumstances."

"But, Sister Agatha, this discovery is critical! Surely, these are minor considerations," Hombardt began.

"Wait, Doctor Hombardt," the nun held up her hand. "I would like to approve the expedition." She took a deep breath.

"It's a risk, but I believe that it will be extremely valuable for the school."

Sister Agatha folded her hands on the desk like a student in detention and said quietly, "if we don't take risks in this world, how can we accomplish anything?"

Hombardt smiled.

"However," she continued," provided I can raise the necessary funding, I will approve this expedition only on one other condition."

"What is it?" Hombardt asked eagerly.

"You are accompanied by John Maletesta."

"Maletesta?" Hombardt said, unbelievingly.

"The English teacher?" Willis joined in.

"The same," Sister Agatha replied. "He's seen combat in the Pacific…in the jungle. That's why we need him in Borneo."

The nun rose from the desk and began walking to the door.

"You can't be serious," Hombardt blustered. He was walking after her. "An English teacher on an expedition like this? Are you joking? Besides, he a…a…"

"Cripple?" completed Willis.

"A boor," Hombardt clarified.

"He's also has a very short temper, and…" Willis began.

Sister Agatha stopped and turned.

"Gentlemen, this discussion is over. I will speak with Mr. Maletesta. Happy hunting."

As Sister Agatha closed the door on the fuming Hombardt and Willis, she thought briefly about whether she should notify her superiors in New York about the plan, but decided against it.

THREE

San Francisco

"Who's next? Who's next? Ahh…Gianni! Step right up, Mister Maletesta! Step right up!" Alfredo Pezzi bellowed.

Pezzi beamed as he watched John Maletesta approach the waiting barber chair. He remembered the time he had given "little Gianni" his first real haircut, while his mother stood by apprehensively. Now he saw a grown man, but something had changed. The barber was more comfortable now with the missing arm than he was a year ago, but not with the things he saw sometimes in Maletesta's deep-set eyes.

"So, Gianni, a little off the top, a little off the sides, a little off the back and all the girls will chase you, huh!" Alfredo laughed as he pulled the sheet over Maletesta.

"So what happened to you, Fredo? You got a little off the top," said Munoz, a regular who was getting his hair cut in the next chair. The regulars could talk like that to Alfredo. Alfredo's head shone brightly in the wall mirrors of the shop, and no one in the neighborhood could remember when it had hair on it. Some said he shined it every morning with olive oil and a cloth.

"You guys with hair," Afredo said as he ran his hand over his head, "you don't know nothing. Girls go crazy to see the shape of a man's head!"

He pulled in his ample stomach and laughed again. The air was punctured by the aroma of garlic. Maletesta joined in the laughter.

The Tip Top barber shop was located on Union Street a few doors down from Van Ness Avenue. It was long and narrow with a single entry door and a large front window looking out onto the street. On that Saturday morning, all four chairs of the

Tip Top were occupied and eight men were waiting in the chairs along the wall opposite the barbers.

The Tip Top was the neighborhood's clearing house of news, deals, and ideas. In the rear of the shop, there was an animated discussion about the fate of the Democrats in the next election and in the middle, a lively exchange on race horses. A thin old man every Saturday whether he needed a haircut or not. He loved bank robbers and lived in the disappointment that all of his favorites were either dead or in prison.

"Now you take Pretty Boy Floyd..." the old man began, to nobody in particular.

"He was a hayseed!" grumbled a man with a hot towel over his face. "Capone would have had him for breakfast!"

"You look out your window on a clear day, mister, and you can see the penthouse in the Bay where your Capone spent five years," the old man rejoined to a burst of laughter from nearby customers.

The conversations continued over Alfredo's selected music. A table model record player was perched on a shelf on the back wall, automatically dropping 78's of Benny Goodman and Beniamino Gigli onto the turntable. The Tip Top clientele called it "music by the two Bennies." No other records were allowed. The barber in the last chair re-stacked the records after they played, and the music blended with the buzzing and clicking of electric clippers and scissors. The aroma of cigarette smoke was overwhelmed by that of talcum, hair oil and after-shave lotion. No cigars or pipes were allowed.

John Maletesta lived in a three story apartment building on Gough Street two blocks from the Tip Top. Unlike his parents who had moved from North Beach to the quieter, foggier Ingleside District, he preferred to stay in the busier and warmer Marina neighborhood where he was only a bus, streetcar, or train away from anywhere in the City, the peninsula, or Oakland.

Earlier that morning Maletesta had tried once again to tie his shoelaces. He had stacked books on a chair under the kitchen table and attempted to pinch one end of the shoelace against the underside of the table. It didn't work. He cursed and kicked the books off the chair.

Then he picked them up and placed them on the table, slipped into his loafers, and walked down three flights of stairs and out through the lobby into the street. As he walked to Alfredo's, the smell of Saturday morning was in the air.

"Hey, Gianni, *ma dormi*? You in there?" Alfredo was in front of the chair, peering at him.

"Yeah. Sorry, Fredo, I guess I was day dreaming."

Shit, even a kid can tie his own shoes. A four-year-old kid can tie his own shoes. And play baseball.

"So," Alfredo continued cutting, "what do you think?"

"About what?" Maletesta asked.

"About this Black player the Dodgers have in the minors, Robinson. Do you think they'll bring him up?"

"I think so. From what I've read, he's great...hitting, fielding, stealing..." Maletesta replied.

"Yeah, those people are great at stealing," a voice interrupted, "that's why they don't belong in baseball!"

The voice belonged to a red-faced man waiting in a chair by the door. He was well-dressed and not known to the regulars. Pandemonium broke out in the shop. Customers and barbers shouted over each other about Black players and the major leagues. One barber jumped into the fray with a story about his cousin who got into a fight with a Black guy in the shipyards. The old man tried to add something about bank robbers in Harlem, but no one paid attention.

"Wait a minute! Wait a minute!" Alfredo shouted, waving his arms. "This is my shop!

I'm the only one who can yell in here. Shut up! Everybody shut up!"

The shop grew quiet and everyone who had gotten up returned to their chairs.

"That's better. Now. We're going to settle this thing with what they call 'expert opinion.' In this chair," he gestured grandly to Maletesta, who rolled his eyes in an appeal to heaven, "we've got Gianni Maletesta, who knows more baseball than any of us. Didn't I myself see him go four-for-five against Cal and pull down a sure homerun over the centerfield fence? Mister Maletesta, what is the verdict?"

With a flourish, Alfredo swept his arm toward John.

The place was silent with the exception of a "yeah Johnny!" from the barber on the end. He simultaneously pulled up the armature on the record player and Beniamino Gigli's voice stopped in mid-aria.

Maletesta was lost in thought again.

Can they play baseball? Jesus. The 93rd gave a hell of an account of themselves on Bougainville before we hit Leyte. Black unit, yeah, it was a Black unit.

"Well," he said, clearing his throat, "they play with the white players in the off season . . . and often beat them. I don't see any reason they shouldn't play during the regular season. Makes sense to me."

There were murmurs of agreement and disagreement in the shop.

"And, there's another thing," Maletesta added, "they fought for their country. Some of them never came back. How can we tell them you can't play baseball here?"

"Who the hell are you?" the red-faced man asked.

He stood up in front of Maletesta's chair.

"What makes you an expert?" he snarled. "I never heard of you! Why aren't you in the majors if you're so good?" He jabbed his index finger at the sitting Maletesta.

Maletesta stood up quickly, the sheet falling to the floor and revealing his missing arm. His eyes were burning, and his right fist was clenched.

"Want to take this outside?" he rasped out.

The red-faced man hesitated.

"*Bastardo!*" Alfredo yelled, who came around from the back of the chair flashing a straight razor. "You get the hell out of my shop, mister, now, you son of a bitch!"

"I can handle this, Fredo!" Maletesta snapped at the barber and took a step forward.

The red-faced man looked into Maletesta's eyes and then at the empty sleeve, confused. He glanced at the rest of the shop and saw the hostility in the faces. He backed toward the door and grabbed the door knob.

"You damned wops are the same as the Blacks!" he yelled as he banged the door and walked quickly down the street.

A young man near the door jumped up from his seat and started toward the door, but a fat man in a yellow shirt called out, "Sit down, Archie!" The young man went back to his chair and the fat man returned to scowling at the *Ring* magazine he was holding. Tony Zale, the *Ring* magazine Fighter of the Year was on the cover.

"I'm sorry, Gianni," Alfredo apologized, "such a thing to happen in my shop...*chi il bastardo...*"

"*Va bene*, Fredo," Maletesta shrugged, looking into the mirror, "that's a terrific haircut!"

The conversations started up again, newspapers were reopened, and Beniamino Gigli resumed singing where he had been interrupted. Maletesta paid for his haircut and bid an embarrassed goodbye to his well-wishers. He left the Tip Top and set off down the street to the bakery on the next block. He stopped at the corner to let some early morning drivers through the intersection before crossing. His remembered that he needed to correct about six more student essays on importance of Edgar Allen Poe before Monday.

"Young man! A moment, please!"

Maletesta turned and saw the man who had been sitting next to him in the barber shop approaching. He was a compact Filipino in his mid-sixties who walked with an agile gait.

"Mister...uh...Munoz, isn't it?" Maletesta asked.

"Yes. Enrique, please," the man replied.

Munoz motioned in conspiratorial fashion for Maletesta to join him in the empty doorway of the building on the corner. He wore a light windbreaker and his right hand was in his pocket.

"They said that you fought the Japanese invaders in my country," Munoz asked when he was closer. "This is true?"

"Yes, on the island of..."

"You have a strong spirit, young man," Munoz interrupted. "As I did when I was your age. It is a good thing, but sometimes can get you into trouble! You have seen one of these before?"

Munoz had withdrawn his hand from his jacket pocket and held it in front of Maletesta. Across his palm lay an oddly beautiful metal object which looked like two engraved silver tubes hinged on one end.

"Sure," Maletesta answered, "it's a butterfly knife. Our scouts carried them. Pretty nifty."

"Good. You know the knife and how it works."

Munoz quickly closed his hand and flicked his wrist. In a trice, the tubes parted to become the handle of a thin bladed knife.

He flicked again and the blade disappeared back into the folded tubes.

"It is now yours," he said, pushing the knife into Maletesta's pocket.

"No, no!" Maletesta protested. "I can't accept this. It's much too valuable."

He began reaching into his pocket to retrieve the knife. A hand gripped his arm firmly and held it. He looked into Munoz' face.

"It is not much reward for one who has lost so much in my country. Please," Munoz insisted.

"All right." Maletesta saw the intensity in Munoz' eyes.

"Thank you."

Munoz suddenly chuckled.

"I too fought invaders when I was your age. Do you know who they were? Americans! Many years ago. We lost that time, but the next time, we will be free. It is as sure as the movement of the sun across the sky."

"I…uh, hope so," Maletesta said, slightly perplexed.

Munoz chuckled again and patted Maletesta on the cheek.

"Good luck, my young friend," he said and then turned and strode back toward Van Ness Avenue without a further word.

Maletesta watched him for a few minutes and then walked over to the bakery.

FOUR

Burlingame

The globe was spinning, a golden blur on its own invisible axis. Sister Agatha stood back to admire it as it slowed. The globe was magnificently detailed in color and raised contours, and it stood in its mahogany carriage next to the door in her small office on the second floor of the Administration Building.

"Thank you, Uncle Con," she whispered. She had developed a habit of quietly talking to herself when she was agitated or contemplative. Growing up in a large boisterous Irish family, Agatha had found it difficult during her "quiet time" studies as a novice. To keep from bursting at the seams and violating the strict rules, she resorted to whispering her thoughts.

As the globe slowed, the oceans of the world emerged, then the lands, and finally the borders—dark lines delineating borders. Sister Agatha gave the globe another slight push. She preferred it as land and water. Borders got in the way of things.

The Angelus had rung some time ago. The campus outside was quiet. There were not many students about on this Saturday afternoon. They had either gone home for the weekend or were studying in their rooms.

Abruptly, she left the globe and went to sit at her desk. She looked at the watch-fob pinned to her sleeve. John Maletesta was due here in a few minutes.

"Ah, you're the clever one, aren't you, Aggie dear," she murmured as she sorted the manila folders on her desk. "Almost all the pieces in one place. And the money. Who'd have thought of the Building Restoration funds? Too clever by far, Aggie. Gambling? No, no-- gambling on a sure thing is not gambling. The Lord knows that."

27

She began to tunelessly sing her mother's old song, the limerick that they all loved because it never made any sense. The melody was lost between generations some time back.

"I saw a hawk in Dundalk
And he mending old shoes,
And a skylark wearing spectacles
And he reading the news."

She opened one of the folders in front of her and tipped out the yellowed newspaper clippings Uncle Con had given her. She sifted through them. A newspaper photo of a laughing young man riding on the shoulders of his boisterous team mates. Another one of him holding a bat over his head in triumph. Box scores with impressive numbers. She removed her eyeglasses and rubbed her eyes. Then she replaced them and read one of the clippings.

"...centerfielder Maletesta again demonstrated why he is the runaway favorite for All-Conference Most Valuable Player this year. He made two spectacular running catches at the fence and was three for four at the plate, including the game-winning home run. Batting coach Tom Brady told this reporter, 'You mark my words, you're looking at the next DiMaggio. I wouldn't be surprised if the Seals weren't considering a tryout for him right now...."

Sister Agatha put the clippings back into the folder and returned it to the pile.

"And then the war," she whispered. "Those terrible battles. My God! His arm gone. Baseball gone forever."

But now he was teaching at All Saints.

"Thank you, again, Uncle Con," she repeated, remembering how the old longshoreman who gave her the globe had met Maletesta at the VA hospital and told her about him. Twice a week, Uncle Con entertained the vets with his accordion, playing sing-along songs, Irish reels, and tunes that were hits twenty years ago.

Maletesta read books throughout these sessions, raising his head only long enough to scowl at Con or the other vets. Con was undeterred, and eventually the two of them began a series of conversations about Maletesta's future and how he would support himself. That dialogue led to a job offer from Sister Agatha who needed teachers for the curriculum changes she was making at the school.

She heard a dog barking outside on Commons. She knew it was Carmen, the stray Labrador/shepherd mix who had adopted Maletesta and followed him around the campus. Then she heard the door open downstairs.

"Stay, Carmen, stay. Good dog. Stay."

It was Maletesta's voice.

Suddenly she heard a crash, the sound of what must have been one of the side tables in the hall going over. Heavy footsteps banged down the hall in probable pursuit of the dog.

"No! Bad dog! Come, Carmen, come! Come!"

Now there were shrieks emanating from the laundry room where three novices were doing the weekly wash.

"Come, damn it! Oh, excuse me..." Maletesta was shouting. The shrieks were replaced by giggles. Finally Sister Agatha heard the entry door slam and a single bark of protest from Carmen outside.

"Two semesters of teaching," Sister Agatha reflected as she closed the folder and waited. "Mister Maletesta has turned out far better than I expected--an imaginative and inspiring young man--but still full of anger and unseen demons." She sighed. "And now something new for him. Will he or won't he? Well, I have no other choice. We'll see."

There was a knock at the door.

"Come in."

The door opened and John Maletesta entered, a smile on his face but a curious look in his eyes.

"Good afternoon, Sister Agatha," Maletesta opened. "A student brought your note to me in the cafeteria. Is something wrong?"

"No, no, John," she smiled. "Please sit down. I have a proposition for you and I'd like you to listen to all of it before you answer. It is a matter which is very critical to the future of the school."

Maletesta slumped into one of the straight-backed chairs opposite Sister Agatha's desk. He shook a cigarette out of a pack of Raleighs and lit it with a battered Zippo. Sister Agatha opened a bottom drawer and brought out a ceramic ashtray shaped like Alcatraz. She placed it on the corner of the desk.

He looked at the ashtray and tried unsuccessfully to control a smile.

"I won it in Skee-ball at Playland," she apologized. "Do you know Doctor Hombardt in Anthropology?"

"We've spoken a few times. The weather, holidays coming . . . that sort of thing. Not a real friendly guy."

"To put it mildly," she agreed. "However, I believe he's come up with something."

Sister Agatha reached around to the bookcase behind her and came back with a yellow and white *National Geographic* magazine. She laid it on the desk and opened it to a to a two-page map of Borneo.

Maletesta leaned forward.

"Borneo," she said quietly. "Thousands of square miles of jungle, mountains, forests, and plains unseen and untouched by what we call civilization."

Her eyes shone behind the glasses, as her finger traced lightly on the page around the interior of the island. "Species of plants and animals uncatalogued by scientists. A place from pre-history. Deep. Hidden. Protected from the ax and the saw and the bulldozer."

She paused and took a long breath.

Maletesta waited, sensing he was not to interrupt. He casually blew a smoke ring at the corner of the desk, but his eyes were watchful.

"Possibly the birthplace of what we consider modern man," she said. Then she chuckled.

"Not the Garden of Eden, of course, although the scenery certainly fits."

Maletesta said nothing.

"Like the French theologian, Robidoux, I accept evolution and the Garden of Eden alike. A spiritual Adam, as it were. Does that surprise or shock you? It's not a popular opinion in the Order."

"No," he said guardedly, stubbing out his cigarette. He wondered where this conversation was going.

"However," Sister Agatha continued, "One does what one has to do. So, are you familiar at all with the search that scientists have been conducting for the physiological first man?"

"You mean, like the Missing Link?" Maletesta asked, following her words carefully.

"Yes, in the popular mind, it's an apt title. I personally believe it was at that juncture in evolution that the Creator imposed the soul in Man. Scientifically, it's when we can find a being who is a thinking tool-maker and user."

Sister Agatha opened a file on the desk which Maletesta could see contained an old newspaper clipping, some photographs and typewritten sheets. He craned his neck to see them better.

"For the past fifty years," she began, "the search has been centered in the Far East."

She was lecturing to him, which would have irritated him had he not become intrigued by her presentation. He sat up a little straighter in the chair.

"It all started with Darwin, of course," Sister Agatha continued, "the discovery of Neanderthal Man in Germany inspired the scientific community to search for the oldest primitive man who was not an ape. Darwin thought that man's origin would be found in Africa with his nearest ancestors--the gorillas, apes, and monkeys.

"A Dutch doctor named Dubois reasoned that there were as many simian types in Asia, so he started looking on the island of Java in the 1890's. Within a year, he found some fossils which became known as Java Man. Java Man made and used fire," she leaned forward and spoke slowly, "That's important...and...he was older than Neanderthal Man."

She was momentarily lost in thought as she stared at the newspaper clipping. Memories came flooding back from years ago when the young nun had hidden it in her hymnal.

"Then, about seventeen years ago," she began, tapping the index finger of her right hand on the yellowed clipping, "a team of scientists found a skull cap and then the fossils of forty people in a dig near Peking, China..."

"China?" Maletesta interrupted.

"Yes, Peking Man, China," Sister Agatha repeated, "the search was narrowing."

She spread the photographs on the desk and handed one to Maletesta. He looked at it. It was an entrance to a cave in what appeared to be the side of a mountain. The other photographs were pictures of the same mountain from different perspectives.

"Where are these from?" Maletesta asked.

"Borneo."

"Who took them, and why are they important?"

"They're Doctor Hombardt's little buried treasure," the nun replied. "He was at one of those outdoor adventure conventions in San Diego--you know the kind: treks in the Gobi Desert, boat rides down the Amazon. Sporting goods manufacturers and travel agencies put them together for armchair adventurers who are almost ready to bolt, but don't."

"Like the annual boat show at the Cow Palace."

"Exactly. Anyway, here he was at this San Diego convention collecting brochures, chatting with guides and the like, and he came upon a large worldwide exhibit of photographs."

She gestured to the photographs.

"These were for sale," the nun continued. "They were part of a batch which had been donated by a travel agency. Photos sent to them by free-lancers in hope of a sale."

Maletesta peered at them.

"Too grainy for a tourist's brochure."

"That's what the agency told Hombardt when he asked. He found out that they were taken by a French freelance photographer before the war. The agency wired him for more, but the unfortunate man drowned in a boating mishap shortly afterward. Then came the war, and the photos gathered dust in a bin of unsolicited material. Eventually, the agency donated the whole bin to be sold at the exhibition. Hombardt bought them in an envelope marked simply 'Borneo.'"

"What's so special about them?"

Sister Agatha turned three of the photographs over. There was faint handwriting on the backs of two of them and a crude map on the third.

"How's your French?" she asked Maletesta.

Maletesta laughed.

"'Come with me to zee Casbah,'" he intoned, mimicking the movie star, Charles Boyer.

"Very funny."

"What does it say?"

Maletesta moved his chair closer to the desk and squinted at the backs of the photographs.

Sister Agatha watched him and said slowly, "It says, 'where I found the human fossils.'"

Maletesta whistled.

"Does it fit?" he asked the nun.

"Like an old shoe to an old sock," Sister Agatha answered. "Studies have shown that the limestone caves of Borneo could provide an extremely rich site for anthropological investigation. These caves are very likely to contain discoveries that are critical to understanding the evolution of man."

He leaned forward and slowly crushed out the cigarette.

"Why have you collected all this stuff, Sister?" he asked.

"The school is mounting an expedition to Borneo."

Maletesta's eyebrows went up.

"The school?" he scoffed. "Who's that? The Department of Anthropology? Hombardt and that fat guy...what's his name...Willis? You've got to be kiddin'."

"I am not 'kidding,' John," she replied coldly. "And I want you to accompany them..."

"No."

She continued speaking as he she had not heard his answer.

"...accompany them and help the School. It's the sort of thing that can put All Saints on the academic map . . ."

"No. Sorry. I've done my tour of duty overseas." He paused and added, "And look what I got for it."

He reached over to his left side, held up the empty sleeve and then let it drop.

"Wouldn't be much use to you there, would I?"

For almost a full minute, the only sound in the room came from the ticking of the Regulator clock on the wall.

"John, I understand," she began, leaning forward, "but surely you see can how important this expedition is to the college."

Maletesta didn't answer. He shook out another cigarette, lit it, and loudly snapped the Zippo shut. He inhaled and blew a smoke ring at the floor.

"Are we finished?" he asked, looking up.

Sister Agatha stood up behind the desk, her eyes blazing.

"We need this expedition, Mister Maletesta! We will not continue to be known as a charm school for the children of the wealthy! These students deserve better..."

She held up a fist and began opening one finger at a time.

"If we find these fossils, we'll have grants...a proper laboratory...modern books...a postgraduate division!"

Maletesta squirmed but said nothing.

She sat down, collected herself and began speaking quietly.

"John, Doctor Hombardt cannot do it alone. They'll be lost or dead within twenty-four hours of leaving the last town. You're the only one I have who knows the jungle, the only one who has been in dangerous situations. I need you to, well, chaperone, as it were. You could call it a job as a guardian angel if you like."

Maletesta raised his right eyebrow and scowled.

"No. I won't. That's final." He turned in the chair to leave.

"Do you like mysteries?" the nun abruptly asked.

"What?"

"Do you like mysteries?"

Maletesta frowned, confused.

"You mean, like three persons in one God?"

The nun laughed.

"No, I mean like 'did the butler do it?'"

"Oh. Sure. Sure. Nero Wolf, Agatha Christie. Yeah, I read quite a few in the hospital. There wasn't much else to do there. Look out the window, I suppose."

Maletesta stubbed the cigarette on Alcatraz and stared at the ceiling.

Sister Agatha said nothing while turning over some pages in another file. She stopped when she came to a letter. She held it up.

"From Robidoux."

"The theologian?"

"Anthropologist and theologian…Jesuit, as a matter of fact. He was part of the team of scientists who discovered the fossils which became known as 'Peking Man.' Do you know what happened to those bones?"

"No." Maletesta tried to appear uninterested.

"They disappeared. Mysteriously."

She relished the curiosity appearing on the young man's face in spite of himself.

"When the Japanese were closing in," she continued, "the Chinese scientists at the Peking

Union Medical College decided to pack up the discoveries and ship them to America for safe-keeping. The fossils were packed in crates; the USS President Harrison awaited them in the harbor at Chinwangtao; a detachment of Marines escorted the cargo to their base to stay overnight before boarding the Harrison. The problem is, you see, they never arrived."

"At the ship?"

"That's right."

"Surely there are records. From the Marines, from the ship…" Maletesta began.

"The records are muddled and spotty," Sister Agatha interrupted. "When the Japanese overran the city, there was chaos. The Marines guarded the consulate, and the President

Harrison pulled out. No one knew where the crates were until…"

Sister Agatha took off her glasses, polished them with a cloth and put them back on.

"Until?" Maletesta asked, leaning forward.

"Now."

She picked up the letter again. "Robidoux and I have corresponded about theology and evolution since before the war. In his latest letter, he mentions almost as an afterthought that a former French prisoner of war wrote to him that he had unloaded the crates off a Japanese ship in early 1942."

"How did he know what they were?"

"A Japanese officer told him. They weren't expected to live. But he survived and wrote to Robidoux after reading a newspaper story about the disappearance of the Peking Man crates."

"Doesn't he want to do something about it?"

"Robidoux's energies are directed elsewhere now…and it's still a slim lead, but beguiling," the nun answered.

"Where were the crates being unloaded?"

"Sibu. Borneo."

"So," Maletesta frowned, "you're talking about two missions?"

"Yes."

"And," Maletesta added, "if, by some wild long shot in this far-fetched tale, I somehow manage to find those old bones…finder's keepers?"

"No, we return them to their rightful owners in China."

"Right now, they're cutting each other's throats."

"It doesn't matter; we'll give them to a proper authority. Do you understand what an incredible accomplishment this expedition will be?"

"I still think we should sell whatever we find," Maletesta answered, grumpily.

"So you've agreed then?"

Maletesta got up and opened the door. He was half-way into the hall, and then he stopped and came back.

"Sister Agatha, I'll call you tomorrow night, all right?"

"All right," she replied, "Goodbye, John."

"He's hooked," she mumbled as the door closed and she put the files back in the cabinet. "A tough one, though. Just what we need."

FIVE

San Francisco

Maletesta drove slowly and carefully through the curves on Highway 1, heading south alongside the Pacific Ocean. His family helped him purchase the 1939 Oldsmobile when he was released from the VA hospital. It had an automatic transmission and a knob on the steering wheel which made driving possible for a one-armed man. Handling the knob was a tricky affair, but, except for a few problems at first, he was able to manage driving quite well.

Before heading south, he had dropped by his parent's home for Sunday lunch. It was one of those rare crisp days in the Ingleside, a bright sunny morning with no overcast. Joe Maletesta, his father, was in the front yard, spiking the lawn with a three-pronged steel spiking tool he had made on the old forge at work. Joe was an iron worker in a shop on Bay Street.

The next door neighbor, Lionel Hatfield, was carrying out his quarterly trim of his lawn. Hatfield, a long-retired stage actor, had a unique method of grass control. Just about every three months, he embarked upon the lawn on his knees with scissors in hand and an empty five gallon oil can alongside him. For almost a week, he would spend an hour a day clipping the grass and weeds shorter than a sheep could crop it. Then, abruptly, he would stop with less than half of the job done and retreat back into his house until the next quarter. Occasionally he emerged for short walks around the neighborhood.

"Hello, Mister Hatfield," Maletesta called to him from the sidewalk where he had parked the Oldsmobile. "How are you today?"

Hatfield looked up from his labors and squinted. He had a wild fringe of white hair around the sides and back of his head. The blue eyes of a baby gazed vacantly at Maletesta.

"Fine and fit as a guardsman, William, fine and fit!" he answered back in a booming voice.

"Nice day, isn't it?"

"Indeed! And how is your father, William? I haven't seen him extant lately."

Hatfield looked vaguely at John's father working next door, but there was no recognition in his eyes.

"Oh, he's doing quite well, Mister Hatfield, quite well," Maletesta replied, unconsciously falling into the old man's cadence.

"Lionel, it's time for tea." A wizened little woman poked her head out of the front door.

"Oh, hello, John," she said when she noticed Maletesta.

"Hello, Mrs. Hatfield."

Lionel arose from his knees and trundled toward the house.

"All's well that ends well, William, all's well that ends well."

Maletesta watched the old man wobble up the stairs before he walked across the lawn to where his father was busy spiking. The house was freshly-painted and blue and purple irises peeked around hydrangea shrubs in the front garden. A row of abalone shells set in concrete delineated the garden from the lawn.

Joe Maletesta was about his son's height but had the thick shoulders and arms of an ironworker. His big hands gripped the four-foot-long spiker on the end of the handle, and he raised it about a foot off the ground. Then he plunged the three prongs into the lawn and pushed the handle back and forth several times to loosen the sod. He pulled it out, moved a few steps, and repeated the procedure. He gave out a small grunt each time the tool hit the ground. It had taken him forty minutes to cover half the lawn. He smiled when he saw his son approaching.

"Hi, Pop."

"Hi, John," Joe said, grunting, "how's the teacher?"

"OK, but I got a new assignment."

"Oh?"

Another small grunt followed. Circles of sweat darkened Joe's light blue chambray shirt under his armpits and beads appeared on his forehead.

"I'm going overseas again," John said lightly.

"What do you mean?"

He stopped the spiker in mid-air and turned to face his son.

"An expedition in the jungle. The school wants me to help look for some prehistoric bones."

"Bones? Whose bones? Where?"

Joe had stopped spiking and was frowning at his son.

"The island of Borneo. It's near…" John began.

"I know where the hell it is! You think I can't read a map? Just because I didn't go to college?"

Joe slammed the spiker into the lawn and the ground trembled slightly.

"You can't go," Joe said, "not anymore. Enough is enough!"

He jerked the spiker out of the lawn and slammed it down again.

"Pop," John said, "I told Sister Agatha I'd let her know tonight for sure. I'm going down to the range, and then I'll decide."

"I know you, Gianni, like the inside of my own hand. You've already made up your mind."

Joe paused and leaned on the handle of the spiker.

"Why do you do this thing? For what? You haven't given enough already?"

41

"Given enough?" John exploded. "What do you think this is? Some kind of penance from the priest? Now I'm ready for heaven?"

"Gianni…"

"Don't give me that Gianni crap!" John was now pacing on the lawn. "This is not some cross to bear! I'm not going to sell pencils on Market Street or end up cutting the lawn with a scissors like the mad Hatfield!"

"Teaching is not selling pencils!"

Joe slammed the spiker back into the lawn. Their raised voices alerted a collie down the street who began to bark.

"And leave that old man out of this," Joe whispered, lowering his voice. "You used to have respect."

There was a silence between them. One stood and stared belligerently at the house across the street. The other resumed the methodical spiking of the lawn. The only sounds on the street were the thuds of the spiker hitting the ground and the grunts of the man behind the spiker. The collie had been called inside.

"Sorry, pop."

Two more thuds of the spiker.

"Do you want to die, Gianni?"

John looked quickly at his father and then away.

"I don't know, Pop. Maybe."

He watched his son, gripping the handle of the spiker tightly. He could not think of anything more to say. John turned and went into the house to see his mother.

Guilia Maletesta was the beauty of the family, raven-haired and graceful, although the lines in her forehead had grown deeper over the last few years than the smile lines around her eyes. She took great pride in the cleanliness of her home. When she returned from nine o'clock Mass that Sunday, she opened all the windows in the house to air out the smells of furniture polish and disinfectant. Joe had not attended Mass since his son had returned from the Pacific.

Lunch was ready when John came into the kitchen. The small table opposite the stove held a vase of freshly- cut irises, a plate of mortadella sandwiches, and a glass of red wine. He kissed his mother on the forehead and she reached up and pinched his cheek.

"*Buon giorno, mama, come va?*"

"Shh, Gianni, you know how your father feels about talking Italian," his mother said softly as if Joe Maletesta was not out front spiking the lawn.

"Oh, I know. Talk American! Talk American! We're Americans now," Maletesta expounded, imitating his father's voice as he sat down at the table.

"Then he planted all those abalone shells out in the front," he laughed. "Might as well put a big sign on the lawn that says 'Italians live here.'"

Guilia Maletesta frowned at him, so he took a few bites of a sandwich.

"Good, mama, very good."

"Gianni, I don't want you fighting with your father," she said, sitting down in the chair opposite him.

"Aw, he'll get over it . . . talk American! Mama, it makes me remember the time Uncle Tilio and Auntie Marie came over from Italy to visit us. Do you remember?"

"Remember? How could I forget? When Tilio got back home and told everyone what happened, your grandmother wouldn't answer my letters for over two years!"

Maletesta chuckled and began reciting the story again.

"There we were all at the dining room table eating dinner and Uncle Tilio started talking about Mussolini and how good he was for Italy...the trains were running on time, there were no trouble makers from the unions..."

John started to laugh and had to put down his sandwich before he could continue.

"Pop was chewing hard, remember? I could see his jaw moving and that vein in his forehead sticking out. Uh-oh, I thought. Then, all of a sudden, he jumped up and grabbed Uncle Tilio by the ear!"

John could not contain his laughter now. He gulped for control.

"Gianni, it was terrible! You shouldn't laugh," said his mother, but she began to laugh too.

"And," John continued, "then he pulled him off his chair and pushed him out the front door! Tilio was screaming and Auntie Marie was waving her hands and crying '*Dio! Dio!*' And then Pop yelled at Uncle Tilio, 'go back to your God-damned Italy and your God-damned dictator if you think he's so God-damned good!' Then he threw his hat down the stairs at him!"

Mother and son fell into gales of laughter at the thought of it all. After the laughter subsided, they discussed his teaching job. He had decided not to tell her about Borneo yet.

"And your students," she asked, "are they nice? Do they respect my boy? No throwing things behind your back?"

"Oh, Mama," John said, "this is college! Everyone pays attention in class. Not like high school."

"So their mamas don't have to come and pick them up because they threw something at somebody when the teacher wasn't looking?" There was a twinkle in her eyes.

"Mama, it didn't happen that often!"

"Mrs. Maletesta," she intoned in a stagey deep voice, "your son has gotten himself into serious trouble this time!"

"So, what's he done, set the place on fire?"

She giggled, her eyes bright with the memory. John looked sheepish at first and then joined in the laughter.

"Annemarie came by the other day," she said quietly when the laughter ended.

"Annemarie who?"

"Gianni, *bambino* . . ."

"No. And please don't bring her up again."

When John was in the hospital, Guilia Maletesta had come every day. He would awake to find her sitting by the bed, silently saying the rosary, the beads turning over in her fingers. Now he frequently caught her watching him warily when she thought he wasn't looking. He did not know what to do about it. Did she think something was wrong with him? Was something wrong with him?

The Sharp Park Exit road sign snapped Maletesta out of his daydreaming about his parents.

SIX

Sharp Park

The fog was still low but lifting as he negotiated the turn off Highway 1 into the town. Sharp Park was a small town on the coast a half-hour out of San Francisco. There was some fishing, some artichoke farming, and, in one of the canyons back toward the hills, the San Francisco municipal shooting range. Maletesta pulled into the parking lot shortly before two o'clock.

As he crunched across the gravel to the entry gate in the chain link fence, Maletesta surveyed the range. In the Fall before the opening of deer season, the range would be full, every point, or shooting position, occupied by would-be hunters with brand new rifles and seasoned woodsmen with their battered Springfields and lever action Winchesters. Now, it was virtually empty. A few kids from the local high school rifle team on the small bore range, a couple of target pistol shooters dreaming of Camp Perry, and some characters with Civil War rifles clouding the air with black powder every time they touched one off. The fog still held in the pine trees which grew around the range and on the hillside, deadening the echoes of the gunshots.

Maletesta put his head back and took a long, deep breath. He loved the wet morning smell of the pine trees in this place. It had been four years since he was last here.

The range was managed under the sharp, no-nonsense eye of Howard Fraley, a former deputy sheriff from Butte, Montana who was also a part-time electrician. Fraley was a small wiry man who wore rimless glasses and was noted for his battered Stetson and a beat up vest that contained just about every item he needed, from keys, pencils, matches and screwdrivers to a Swiss Army knife and a plug of Day's Work.

There was a small cinder block building in the southwest corner of the range where potential shooters registered, paid fees, bought targets, drank coffee, and talked about guns and hunting. Fishing stories were not allowed.

Metal folding chairs were scattered about, and the walls were covered with old posters from Winchester and Remington. The registration desk was operated by Mrs. Fraley, a diminutive white haired woman who first name no one had ever heard. Once a month she baked corn bread and brought it to the range. Her corn bread had been a favorite of the copper miners in her family and she continued the tradition in California.

When Maletesta entered the building, Howard Fraley was leaning over the registration desk talking to his wife, his back to the door. Maletesta walked up behind him.

"Morning, Howard."

Fraley turned around, took a long look at John, and then grabbed him in a fierce bear hug, his eyes filling up.

"God, boy," he uttered in a barely controllable voice, "it's good to see you!"

Mrs. Fraley had less control. She burst into tears and came running around the desk.

"John, John, praise God, you're home all right," she cried and reached up and kissed him on the cheek. She averted her eyes from the empty sleeve. She and Howard had heard about it from friends.

"Well, missing a wing," John said, after a moment.

He held up the empty sleeve with his right hand and smiled foolishly.

There was an awkward pause, and then Fraley cleared his throat noisily.

"Oh hell, boy," Howard said, "I've always said we've got one too many of everything we have. That's what I've always said. Haven't I, mother?"

"Yes, Howard, that's what you've always said," Mrs. Fraley replied quickly.

"Hell, my cousin Leo lost a lung in the First War; krauts gassed him. But he's still pouring concrete in Butte, ain't he, mother…"

They stood and looked at each other like people on a first date.

"You look as solid as ever, son," Fraley broke the silence, "c'mon, it's time for coffee!"

He led John over to the stained card table which held a huge chromium coffee pot, a variety of mugs and cups, two USN spoons, a bowl of sugar and a bottle of milk.

"Still like it black?" Fraley asked as he turned the faucet to fill one of the mugs.

They sat in the adjacent folding chairs for about twenty minutes, drinking coffee and talking about John's old rifle team in college and the state of the world in 1946. Finally, John brought up the reason why he had returned.

"Howard, I've got a favor to ask."

"You name it, son, you know that."

"I've been asked to participate in what might be a pretty dangerous job. In Borneo. You know, headhunters and stuff like that," said John.

"Yeah? Sounds excitin', what's the problem?"

"Well, if this was a stagecoach in a western, I'm supposed to be the guy riding shotgun. You know, look out for everybody, protect them." Maletesta shifted in his chair in discomfort.

"I don't see any problem in that," Fraley said, "hell, boy, ain't that what you done in the Pacific?"

"I had two arms then."

"So?"

John stood up and walked over to the window looking out on the range. He pointed to a young riflemen firing in the offhand position, rifle butt locked into the shoulder, left hand under the forearm, right hand gripping the trigger, one elbow pointing down, one elbow pointing out. He turned in exasperation.

"How can I defend anybody with one arm? People will be depending on me. I was good with a rifle...I had a good teacher."

Maletesta waved his right hand at the shooters outside.

"Look, Howard...it takes two arms!"

Maletesta sunk down in one of the folding chairs and glared at the concrete floor.

"Hmmm," Fraley murmured.

Fraley placed his cup down carefully on the table. He reached into a vest pocket and scratched a kitchen match on the underside of the table and held it to the tip of the cigar, breathing mightily. Maletesta's nostrils quivered at the familiar smell.

"You're gettin' too riled up, son," he said after a few puffs.

"Howard, you're the only one I know who might have an idea about this."

"I might," Fraley replied. He scratched the bald spot on the back of his head and then blew some more acrid smoke toward the ceiling.

The grayish cloud refused to ascend. It hung in the air over them. Fraley looked at it and then laid the cigar on the edge of the table. He got up and walked back to a pile of non-descript items next to the wall. After pulling off several knapsacks and tarpaulins, he came upon a footlocker.

"Ah ha," he said almost to himself, and, lifting the lid, began rummaging through it.

The first item he pulled out was an old New Service Colt ("too big!" he grunted). Then a .32 lemon squeezer ("OK for close work only"). A Luger ("sure to jam in a jungle!"). He tossed odds and ends of magazines and barrels. Eventually, he turned to Maletesta and held a dull black pistol up in triumph.

Maletesta was watching the foraging curiously.

"A pistol, Howard?" John asked in disappointment.

"Not just a pistol, you ignoraymus, a sure enough Browning Hi-Power! The last design of old John Moses B himself and built in Canada for the British commandos! Inglis is the name on it, but it's a Browning as in U.S.A."

"C'mon," Fraley stood up, grabbed a few extra magazines and a box of ammunition and made for the door.

John caught up with Fraley at the last firing position of the pistol range. The target shooters had left, so they had the range to themselves. There were still targets stapled up out at twenty-five yards. Fraley laid the Browning on the bench and began loading the magazines. John watched in amazement as he continued stuffing the 9 mm bullets into the clips.

"If you're counting," Fraley said, "that's thirteen. According to those books Mrs. Fraley reads, that's too many for dinner," he harrumphed and turned to Maletesta smiling, "but for pistoleros like you and me, that's just enough. Take hold of that Browning, Roy."

"OK, Gabby," John smiled at the familiar allusion to Roy Rogers as he picked up the empty pistol. It felt solid in his hand even though it was thicker than the Colt .45 he had used in the army.

"Put the bottom part of the muzzle against the bench and push."

John placed the underside of the muzzle against the bench and pressed hard. The slide of the pistol retracted and locked.

"Hold the pistol in your left arm pit."

John put the pistol under his left arm pit, gripping it as hard as he could.

"Put one of those magazines in it."

John picked one of the loaded magazines and locked it into the butt of the pistol.

"Now take it out of your armpit, thumb down the slide stop and let fly. And don't let me hear any more of this one-arm bird dung. Coffee at four, Roy."

Fraley walked down the line to where some would-be Daniel Boones were stuffing wadding down the muzzles of Kentucky rifles.

Maletesta emptied the magazine at the 25 yard target, getting the feel of the big Browning. Before the war, he used the classic stance with his right arm straight, one eye closed and one looking down the barrel, and his left hand in his pocket. Now he fired with the gun held chest high, both eyes open, looking at the target. There was no left hand to worry about.

At regular intervals, the voice of little Mrs. Fraley crackled over the loudspeakers mounted on the roof of the range building.

"Ready on the right...ready on the left...load...commence firing."

Maletesta used up the box of cartridges Fraley brought and went back to the clubhouse to buy several more boxes. Several times during the afternoon the magazine clattered to the ground, but only once did he drop the pistol and then only on the bench. He taught himself to laboriously load the magazine by holding it in his left armpit and stuffing the cartridges in, one by one.

Fraley watched him periodically from down range and Mrs. Fraley also took a turn or two at the window.

At four o'clock, his ears ringing, his armpit sore, and his thumb raw, Maletesta met Fraley at the coffeepot.

"Well?" the old man asked.

Maletesta laid the Browning on the table and looked at Fraley.

"It might just work, Howard. I like it. Thanks. How much does it go for?"

Maletesta reached to extract his wallet from his back pocket.

"I'll tell you when you get back. Don't forget, son, always carry it cocked and locked. You don't want to be looking for a table top when trouble pops up. Cocked and locked. And keep a couple of loaded clips with you."

Fraley picked up the pot and poured two cups of coffee, then brought his tool box over the table and picked up the Browning.

"Now sit down, John. I'm gonna fiddle with this a bit so the magazine will drop out easily when you press the release button. While I do that, I want to tell you about this big buck Mrs. Fraley brought down last August up near Whiskeytown. You won't believe it, but I swear it's true. I knew it was gonna be interestin' when she told me she was gonna take that old 38-40 takedown rifle of hers, that one that was new when Buffalo Bill was a pup…"

Later, while Maletesta was driving toward home up Highway 1, he let the Oldsmobile out and tested his control at 70 miles per hour. His nerves were steady. A few miles further up the road he stopped at a roadside stand and bought a bag of artichokes. He filled his lungs with the air of the sea. He watched a fishing boat bobbing in the waves off shore. On an impulse, he reached down, picked up a rock and flung it toward the water. It fell short, thudding silently in the sand. It didn't matter. He knew the answer. He would phone Sister Agatha at six o'clock.

By the time he passed Playland at the Beach, he was whistling an aria from "La Tosca."

SEVEN

Celebes Sea

Sister Agatha was right. It's not exactly the Queen Mary.
Maletesta lay in his bunk listening to the faint hum of the ship's engines. He closed his book and studied the bulkhead.

"Gentlemen, this journey will be a very Spartan affair," Sister Agatha had told them in a meeting the day before they left, "we simply do not have the resources for a luxury cruise. The guide, the equipment, and the provisions have stretched our finances to their limit."

So Hombardt, Willis, and Maletesta sailed out under the Golden Gate Bridge on the Star of Malaya, a tramp steamer of Dutch registry which was serviceable but not far from retirement. There was a three day layover in Honolulu while a bearing was replaced in the ancient engine.

Well, at least she's water tight. Maletesta glanced around his cabin at the rusting seams and corroded rivets. *So far.*

His left arm was suddenly itchy and he put down his book and automatically reached to scratch it with his right hand. But there was no arm where the itch was. It had happened before. He scowled and tossed the book into his open suitcase on the deck. The book was a turn-of-the century account about Borneo that he'd found in a dusty corner of the Holmes Book Store on Second Street.

Maletesta looked at his watch, stretched and sat up. It was eight o'clock, time for the nightly meeting in Hombardt's cabin. As he stood, the Star of Malaya rolled slightly as she negotiated her way through the Celebes Sea west of the Philippines. He corrected his balance easily, having got his sea legs back during the third day out of San Francisco. He slipped on a shoulder holster with the Browning in it, covered it with his linen jacket, and stepped out into the passageway.

Hombardt's cabin was next to the captain's, a result of some generously spread American dollars. Hombardt was upset when he first saw the old tramp steamer on Pier 19 but was confident in his ability to negotiate better circumstances for himself in any situation. Therefore, in addition to accommodations, he had also arranged for such luxuries as ice and refrigerated fruit.

The Star of Malaya was captained by Eduardo Ricardo Lorenzo Cardoza, whose crew called him "the Portagee" behind his back. The crew were hard men from backgrounds nobody questioned. It was an efficient--if homely--ship, and its owners expected their profit margin in the Pacific trade. No questions were asked of the crew members as long as they worked hard and kept their mouths shut. The war was over, and the trade routes were open again. The Star of Malaya was carrying surplus Jeep engines to a middleman in Singapore. Dropping off paying passengers along the way just added to the profit.

Doctor Richard Rossi Hombardt called nightly meetings in his cabin to review the project and give Willis and Maletesta an opportunity to bask in his scholarship. His family owned a vineyard in the Napa Valley and he grew up in the habit of giving orders to lesser beings. Presiding over a class of only two on ship was difficult for him.

As Maletesta entered the cabin, Hombardt was pinning a map of Borneo to the plywood wall opposite the door. The once-proud brass and teak fittings of the cabin were dull, scratched, missing, or replaced with cheaper materials. There was a small teak table under the map where C. Allen Willis sat, sweating and writing in his journal. Willis had a brother who was a surgeon in a San Francisco hospital noted for its quick use of the scalpel to remedy any condition.

The sight of blood drove Willis from medicine to anthropology and, with Hombardt always in the main light, he looked forward to an antiseptic career at university level, recording the learned activities of the great man for posterity.

"Ah, Maletesta," Hombardt purred, as Maletesta sat in one of the two remaining chairs at the table, "right on time! How excellent!"

Maletesta murmured greetings to the two of them and Hombardt continued.

"As I was saying last night, it's quite an easy journey: we land at Sibu, take a ride upriver into the interior, have a little walk in the bush, and, presto, we're at the caves!"

"Doctor, that's some pretty sticky country..." Maletesta began.

"Stuff and nonsense!" Hombardt said, "there's really nothing to be afraid of..."

"Afraid of?" Maletesta blurted darkly.

Willis giggled artificially to clear the air.

"Now, now, John," he said to Maletesta, patting him on the knee, "let's not..."

At that moment there was an ear-shattering report as the center of the door splintered and a bullet smacked into the map. Two more shots were fired rapidly and the door flew open.

In the doorway stood a tattooed and turbaned Malay pirate, holding a broom handle Mauser machine pistol at waist level. He hesitated and smiled at his prizes. Willis had toppled backward in his chair and Hombardt stood frozen in front of the map.

The pirate died instantly as Maletesta's snap shot caught him under his right eye. They could hear more shots and yelling from above.

"Pirates!" Maletesta blurted out and then felt foolish. He holstered the Browning and picked up the dead pirate's Mauser.

He handed it to Hombardt who took it like a robot. Willis was still on the floor covering his ears and babbling something. "Hombardt! Hombardt!" Maletesta shouted. "I'm not deaf!" Hombardt shouted back. "OK," Maletesta said, "You stay here with Willis. Cut the light. Pile what you can against the door. I'm going up to see what's going on!"

Browning in hand, Maletesta stepped slowly out into the passageway. As he poked along the wall, another pirate appeared with a rifle in his hands. Maletesta fired twice and the pirate dropped to the deck groaning. He stepped over him and continued down the passageway. The shouting and firing above was now in competition with the sporadic and heavier sound of machine gun fire.

He climbed carefully up the companionway, leaning against the railing for balance. He looked out onto the deck and saw three pirates firing at the wheelhouse from a position behind cargo lashed to the deck. He rested his arm on the bulkhead and squeezed off a shot. The pistol jumped in his hand and one of the pirates screamed and grabbed his shoulder, dropped his rifle and slipped to the deck in agony.

The other two pirates turned toward Maletesta and fired their Lee Enfields at him. He ducked back into the companionway as the .303 bullets pinged off the steel. He popped out again two feet above the deck and returned their fire. One fell and the other retreated to the other side of the cargo. As he disappeared, Maletesta quickly crossed the deck to the base of the wheelhouse. He heard a slight sound behind him and turned just in time to see a long-bladed parang arcing through the air toward his head. He dropped instinctively, and fired three bullets into the pirate wielding the parang. The pirate fell next to him thrashing and gurgling his last breath.

Another pirate came running down the deck, saw Maletesta, dropped his carbine and jumped over the side.

Maletesta was soaking in sweat. It was running in his eyes, and his hand was wet around the butt of the Browning. Its slide was not locked back, indicating that there were still more rounds in the magazine.

Jesus, it's still loaded. How many left? Pirates? Bullets?

He watched the man dying next to him, and he began to shake uncontrollably. He steadied himself with several deep breaths.

The machine gun fire from the wheel house grew louder and steadier. More pirates were now jumping over board back to their boats. The shouts now were from the crew in triumph, not pirates in attack. Gradually, the shooting stopped. Within minutes the ship was still again, save for the soft roll of the sea.

Maletesta pushed the safety up on the Browning and slid it back into the shoulder holster. He pulled himself to his feet as the captain and two of his crew came down the gangway from the wheelhouse.

"Surprised dose sons of da devil, you can bet on dat!" shouted Cardoza. His eyes were wild and a trickle of blood ran down the side of his face. He laughed maniacally and shook a Thompson submachine gun over his head.

"Som a na bitch! Never t'ought we had dese, huh? Murderers. Cut your throat for copper earrin'!" He paused and saw his first mate stripping the jewelry from one of the dead pirates.

"When you finish, t'row 'em overboard, dead or alive! I don't wanna dat scum on my ship! Feed da fishes!"

Maletesta began walking back to the companionway.

"Hey you, wait!" Cardoza caught up with Maletesta. "Say, Doctor, you done fine job with dat pistol. Got dat bunch was holding us down. You inna war?" Cardoza smiled ingratiatingly.

"Thanks," Maletesta replied, leaning against the bulkhead, "but no doctor. Just a teacher. Yeah, I was in the war."

"Well, you done damn good for a . . . I mean . . ." Cardoza hesitated and once again lifted up the Thompson. "Got dese in Manila. Surplus, like da Jeep engines. Twenny dollar each. Good investment, huh? Som a na bitch!"

Cardoza laughed again and slapped Maletesta on the back. Then he fired a short burst into the air which brought several of his crew running to the shots. They all laughed when they saw Cardoza waving the Thompson and headed back to their stations. The shell casings rolled into the scuppers with the blood of the pirates.

Maletesta went down the companionway and walked slowly toward Hombardt's cabin. For no apparent reason, his left arm ached unceasingly. There was a drumming inside his head, and he was beginning to distrust his legs.

He knocked on the door of Hombardt's cabin and received a string of Mauser bullets in return, splintering the door and ricocheting around the passageway. He flattened himself against the wall.

"Who is it?" Hombardt's voice screamed out from inside the cabin.

"Jesus Christ!" Maletesta swore, "don't you think you could have asked that first? It's Maletesta. You know, M a-l-e-t-e-s-t-a!"

There was a sound of scraping from within and in a few minutes, the door, shattered and splintered, opened. Hombardt stood there, Mauser in hand, defiance in eye.

"You certainly took your time, Mister Maletesta! When I agreed with Sister Agatha to allow you on the expedition, it was as a personal bodyguard. My work is important! My life was in danger, and where were you?"

Hombardt took another breath.

"Saving your own skin? Hiding? Playing war games again?"

Maletesta gagged and began to speak.

"Never mind the excuses! It will all be in my report! Good night, Mister Maletesta."

With that, Hombardt pushed the shattered door shut.

Maletesta stood for a moment at the door, stunned. His hand went to the Browning and then stopped. He took a slow, deep breath and walked back down the passageway to his cabin, leaning into the rolls of the Star of Malaya as it continued its passage through the Sulu Sea around the northern tip of Borneo. He fell into his bunk and lay awake for over an hour, sweating and shaking. Newsreel images of burning bunkers and Japanese soldiers seared the inside of his eyelids and the screaming would not leave his ears. Finally, he fell into a deep and dreamless sleep.

EIGHT

New York City

The Superior General was pacing again. Short, precise steps, her heels clicking faintly on the parquet floor. The school year had ended for the Order's forty-two grammar schools, high schools, and colleges. Now the fiscal review began. The Superior General was sixty five, thin-faced and thin lipped. It was a muggy summer night in New York City, but the windows were not open in the administrative office. It was hot living in heavy black habits, but she and a younger nun at the table had long ago learned to drive the heat from their minds.

Overall, the Order of the Immaculate Heart's schools were doing quite well. There were always one or two slackers, schools that never seemed to pull their own weight. The Superior General knew that the time would come when she could comfortably and quietly close them. She rarely left New York, so she remained unaffected by the relationship of a school to a community. The schools were ciphers: successful or unsuccessful.

As she paced, she circled a long table laden with ledger books, reports and spread sheets. The other nun, who was the Order's principle bookkeeper, sat at the table, watching the Superior General closely.

"And then there's our western schools," the Superior General opened in her thin voice, "Let's see, the first would be All Saints. How is that one doing?"

She stopped pacing and turned to the bookkeeper at the end of the question. The bookkeeper picked up the ledger book in front of her. She peered at the columns.

"It appears," she replied, nodding, "that donations and admissions have both increased."

"Good. Who runs that one?"

"Agatha Buckley."

"Ah, yes. Sister Agatha. I believe you know her?"

"We grew up in the same parish in San Francisco."

"Did you? What parish? I was assigned to Saint Brigid's in San Francisco many years ago."

"St. Paul's in the Mission District."

"Oh," the Superior General said, pursing her lips. "But neither you nor Sister Agatha sound like anyone I've met from the Mission District. Those people have an odd habit of adding 'r's to words like 'idea' and subtracting them from words like 'mirror,'" she laughed, "so someone has an 'idear' and looks in the 'mirro.' Sometimes I thought I was in Brooklyn!"

"Yes," the bookkeeper added primly, "and they don't pronounce their 't's. They say 'budder,' instead of 'butter.' *Lazy lips*, my mother called it. My mother's family was from Pennsylvania. Agatha's family was from *Ireland*, as were many of our fellow students," she shuddered, "and they *all* slaughtered the English language."

"Then why doesn't Agatha have that accent?"

"You won't believe this," the bookkeeper answered, relishing the discussion. She put down the ledger book. "When we all came back from summer vacation to begin our senior year at St. Paul's, Agatha's voice had changed. *Everyone* was talking about it. What had *happened*? I asked around and found out from her cousin that Agatha had spent the entire month of July talking with marbles in her mouth!"

"Marbles in her mouth? My goodness!"

"Yes," she nodded. "Her cousin said that Agatha had read it in a book! We all thought it was quite amusing, her talking like she *was somebody*. By the time we were novices, she sounded like Katharine Hepburn, for heaven's sake!"

"Interesting. When did you see her last?"

"About ten years ago. She was carrying on about that pilot, you know, the one who was lost before the war?"

"Wainwright?"

"Yes. Agatha was quite taken with her as *a role model for women*, of all things! She's *really* a one, our Agatha!"

"Role model? Maybe for rule breakers! Anyway, she seems to be doing a good job at All Saints…"

The Superior General's words hung in the air as she looked down at the ledger book on the table.

"It depends on who you speak to," the bookkeeper replied curtly.

"Oh?"

"'I've heard that she's made some enemies in some quarters. I mean, *really now*, what was the purpose of adding all those science and mathematics classes! For young ladies? They say that some parents are *not very happy* about it. Do they *really need* these classes to be a good wives and mothers? That's what *some people* are wondering."

"Hmm . . . well, I'll have to look into that. But you did say that donations and admissions have increased, didn't you?"

"It *appears so* at the present."

"Good. Now, let's consider the situation at Saint Anne's College."

On that same night, three thousand miles away in Burlingame, California, a light rain was falling. The convent at All Saints' was silent, and Sister Agatha was hunched over her desk in her room.

The only sound was the scratch of her fountain pen on the paper, the low ticking of a windup alarm clock and the rasp of her labored breathing. Sister Agatha had a map spread out on her desk and was plotting the journey of the Star of Malaya across the Pacific Ocean. She slid a twelve inch wooden ruler carefully across the ocean and made notations on a sheet of white notebook paper. Periodically, she consulted a calendar on the wall. The final line she drew placed the ship somewhere in the Philippines. She set down her pen and capped it. Then she folded up the map and placed it with the sheet of calculations into a drawer.

She turned the lamp off and began her Rosary.

NINE

Sibu, Borneo

The sun beat down on sweating longshoremen as they offloaded the Star of Malaya. The crates of anthropological equipment, camp stores, canned food, testing gear, and all the paraphernalia necessary for the trek and the four-month dig were being lowered to the dock and then loaded onto ancient Ford drayage trucks which carried the cargo to storage in the warehouses on the river across town.

Sibu. Borneo. An inland port which was the gateway to the interior of Sarawak province. An abandoned and scuttled Japanese gunboat lay in the water not far from the Star of Malaya. The town was too busy returning to normal to worry about a water-logged Japanese ship. The Japanese were gone. That was what was important. There were two other small freighters like the Star which navigated the Rejang river to Sibu, several junks, and a number of skiffs and trimarans along the waterfront.

The unlikely trio from the College of All Saints stood on the dock watching their cargo being unloaded. Willis had a clipboard and was making serious check marks on it as each item descended from ship to the dock. Hombardt stood with his back straight and looked out over the longshoremen, the waterfront, and the town in general. Maletesta watched the diverse crowd on the dock absentmindedly. His thoughts were his own.

Hombardt and Willis had both donned .38 Enfield revolvers in canvas flap holsters to accompany their Frank Buck outfits of khaki and pith helmets. Hombardt had also somehow procured a British officer's swagger stick which he used to swat at real and imagined insects as he sauntered along the dock. Maletesta's Browning was under his linen jacket and the sweat ran down his face from the band of his bush hat.

When the cargo was loaded, and the trucks left for their journeys to riverside warehouses,

Hombardt announced that it was time for them to seek out their guide and finalize their agreements. He asked one of the longshoremen for directions to the office of Gustavus Van Vliet and, after drawing a rough map in his notebook, they began walking.

That summer of 1946 in Sibu found a wide diversity of people in town. The streets, such as they were, were awash with hawkers and peddlers selling everything from handmade jewelry and baskets to exotic birds and relics of the headhunters. Herbal doctors sat silently under building eaves with bottles of various plant pieces offering cures for most maladies. The trio paused at a makeshift booth of grisly souvenirs from the headhunters. On sale were a number of ancient skulls and weapons, headhunting having long since abolished by various colonial governments. Hombardt studied the heads with a look of dissatisfaction.

"Willis, it's difficult to believe that prehistoric beings related to these savages may also be our ancestors, and yet my career is balanced right now on this belief," he grumbled. Willis gaped at the heads in horror.

"Savages," said Willis, inadvertently licking his lips.

The seller, missing several teeth and not knowing English, smiled encouragingly. Then he held up one of the heads as an offering to them.

"No wantee! No wantee!" shouted Hombardt as the two backed away from the stall.

Meanwhile, Maletesta was being surrounded by a band of street urchins holding up live turtles and stuffed monkeys and snakes. "Hey, mister! Hey, mister! You buy, huh?" they called.

Maletesta shook his head negative and kept moving. Even the stones in the street felt hot under his feet. Or he imagined them to be hot. He could no longer tell as the trio trudged along, away from the waterfront. A blind woman followed in line for a while but finally gave up. Here and there they felt the stares of people from the interior who could be found in groups of two or three near trade stores looking at once bemused and bewildered. There were Chinese, along with Pacific islanders, people from the interior, a sprinkling of whites, and those mythical people who live in all the port towns of the world. The trio passed families cooking on small braziers in the street and families washing babies in galvanized tubs. Their ears were full of the banging of a blacksmith's hammer, the drone of gas-powered generators, the cacophony of a dozen different dialects.

Hombardt strode doggedly ahead as if on parade. Willis followed, tugging at his collar, blotches of perspiration widening on the jacket under his armpits. Since turning forty, he had gained a bit of weight and the heat bothered him immensely. Maletesta brought up the rear, his mind absorbing everything around him.

Hombardt consulted with the map in his notebook for directions. He turned left at an intersection and pointed to a two story building in the corner a short block away. A sign jutted out over a door to a ground floor office: "Gustavus Van Vliet, Agent and Guide." Two Malays who were lounging in the doorway got up and entered the office as the trio approached.

Inside the office, Hombardt, Willis, and Maletesta found themselves at a battered waist-high wooden counter. Behind the counter, a huge black-haired woman in a flowery print dress sat with her back to them at an equally battered desk, reading a wrinkled copy of Life magazine. Overhead, a ceiling fan revolved lazily, neither creating coolness nor driving off the flying insects. As they stood there at the counter, the woman smashed an insect on the desk with the magazine, and then continued to read. She said nothing.

"Good morning, miss," Hombardt announced crisply.

The woman said nothing.

"*Bon jour mademoiselle*," Hombardt tried again.

The woman turned a page in the magazine.

"*Buenas tardes, senorita?*" Hombardt's face flushed.

"She might be a Samoan," Willis offered. "but I don't know what language they… "

"Try all the languages you want, mate. She's deaf as a stump."

The voice came from a white man who appeared in the doorway to the inner office. He was in his mid-thirties with yellow hair, a yellow mustache, and the red peeling skin of a man who spends a lot of time in the sun and never turns brown.

"Martinus Van Vliet, at your service. Or should I say, Doctor Hombardt, I presume?"

The man laughed heartily at his own joke and motioned the trio to come ahead into his office. Though apparently Dutch, his accent and vocabulary reeked Australia. As they passed the woman, she looked up at them quizzically.

"Valuable woman, one who doesn't talk, what? And, in this business, also one who doesn't hear!" He laughed again. "Break you in two if she don't like you."

Hombardt and Maletesta followed him into the room, with Willis behind, stepping gingerly around the woman.

"Sit down, gentlemen, wherever you can find a seat!"

The inner office was smaller than the street office and loaded with crates of varying sizes. Van Vliet sat at a desk which was cluttered with paper work, bills of lading, invoices, customs certificates, and correspondence. There was also a serviceable Underwood typewriter, an overflowing ashtray, and unidentifiable indigenous objects. On the walls there were pictures of baskets and blowguns, and photographs of grinning white hunters standing next to dead animals. A stuffed leopard head watched marble-eyed from above the desk. Behind Van Vliet, a dark-skinned islander sat impassively on a wooden crate.

Hombardt took the only other chair, Willis and Maletesta found crates at appropriate heights.

"My business is with Gustavus Van Vliet. Can you tell me where he is?" Hombardt asked abruptly. He brought a letter and some documents out of his side pocket and placed them on the desk.

"Sure, no trouble at all, he's dead," Van Vliet answered evenly. He had a twitch on his left temple that appeared every few minutes. His eyes squinted in time with the twitch.

"What? That's impossible! Less than two weeks ago I received a telegram confirming our arrangements. Why, it's all paid!"

Hombardt jumped up and pointed the appropriate places on the papers he had laid on the desk.

"Easy there, mate, easy. Your expedition's still on the burner. Only difference is, Uncle Gus ain't taking you, I am! I know the area in question very well. So does Kwan here."

Van Vliet nodded toward the silent islander. He ran his finger over a map on his desk.

"We scoot up the river, hop through the jungle into the highlands, and there we are at the caves, not far from the old volcano."

"Volcano?" Willis squeaked in alarm.

"Dead as mutton, mate. Like you Yanks say, the whole thing'll be easy as pie."

Hombardt was relieved. He smiled and began putting his papers back into his jacket.

"However," Van Vliet said, "there's a hitch. My paperwork says you're paid for two. Who's staying behind?" He gestured at Maletesta and Willis before his eyes stayed on Maletesta. Then he twitched again and spoke directly to Maletesta.

"I think you ought to spend the time here in Sibu, mate," Van Vliet smiled, "you know, being injured and all, as you are."

Before Hombardt could answer, Maletesta spoke.

"You were paid for three," he said quietly, looking directly into Van Vliet's eyes. Van Vliet flicked his eyes back to Hombardt, who laid a receipt back on the desk.

"You can see that the correct amount has been paid," Hombardt explained as Van Vliet took the paper and studied it.

"Hmm, yes, it appears you're right. Uncle's paperwork got a little wet, don't you know."

"What has happened to Gustavus Van Vliet?" Willis asked.

"Snake. Dead in twenty minutes. Very sad." Van Vliet replied.

Van Vliet stood up to indicate that the meeting was over.

"My man outside will take you to your hotel. Be ready the day after tomorrow at eight in the morning. Good day, gentlemen."

After the trio left, Van Vliet turned to Kwan, his companion.

"That's him. The one-armed bloke. Get rid of him. Tonight."

TEN

Sibu

Cramped. Crowded. Helmets bang against each other. Muscles ache. Crouching. Leg trembles. Too tight. Hang on to carbine, lifeline. Salt spray. Holy Mary, Mother of God. McCarthy. Bump...bump...bump. Each wave under us, closer to the shore. Closer. Closer. Oh God, Simpson's thrown up. I'm gonna be sick. God, what firing from the Navy! OK, no Japanese'll be left. Stomach hurts. Can't swallow. Don't be sick, Gianni. Please God, don't be sick! Think . . . count 1-2-3. Please, don't be sick. The beach. Shit. Gate's down. Hit the beach! "Up! Up! Go! Go!" What? We're in water! Where's the beach? Good. Finally sand. Move, feet! Move, feet! Jesus! Who the hell is firing at us? Thought they'd be dead. Eddie, get up! Eddie, your head! Here, I've got you.

Maletesta writhed in his bed, groaning. He could hear voices calling him from somewhere outside. He kicked off the thin sheet covering him and grabbed spasmodically at the air.

I've got you, Eddie; hang on, man. C'mon, man, we gotta get outta here! C'mon! Eddie! Jesus, Eddie! Medic! Oh God, medic! Oh God! "Move it, lieutenant! Move! Move! Move!" *"Where's his head? Where's his head!"* "Move! Move! Move! He's dead! Godamnit! Move! Move!"

Maletesta jumped up from the bed and stumbled through the mosquito netting. He was soaking in sweat. With unseeing eyes, he looked wildly around for cover.

Where? The trees! Get to the trees!

Suddenly he realized: it was not Leyte Gulf, it was the room at the Hotel Empire in Sibu. He saw the walls, the potted palms in the corner, the dresser with the water basin. Yes, now he knew where he was.

Another dream. He shivered.

71

Shaking, he moved to the wicker chair at the window which overlooked the street. He lit a cigarette and sat down, slowing turning the lighter over and over in his hand. The smoke hung lifeless in the dead air.

The doctors said the dreams would end eventually.

When will they end? What did they know? Doctors. Stateside soldiers. Could care less.

His mind drifted from the inadequate assurances of the VA doctors to the problems and inconsistencies of the present situation.

Martinus Van Vliet. A Dutchman with an Aussie accent. How? Something's odd here.

What happened to Gustavus? A snake? All those crates in the office? Face it, Gianni, the guy's a smuggler and who knows what else? Leave it to Hombardt to find him. Well, I'll have to keep my eyes open.

Outside, the sun was setting. Maletesta decided to go for a walk to clear his mind. He threw on his linen jacket and went downstairs to the desk. He still had two hours left before the nightly meeting. He left a message with the clerk at the desk and hurried out into the street. The Browning was locked inside his suitcase in his room.

There were still people about, though the shops were closing and the peddlers bagging up their wares. He walked along without a goal, aware of the changing scene around him but strangely tuned into a now-familiar interior refrain about his arm and his future.

Future? What future? I'll probably die here. So what?

He hardly noticed that the cobbled streets under him became gravel and the gravel streets became packed dirt as he traversed away from the waterfront.

Some children played in the streets. Old people sat in doorways, hushed conversations and laughter floated in the still air. He passed a cinema where young women stood in line with their mothers. Across the road, young men talked idly, unobtrusively eyeing the girls. Dusk growing darker into night and there were few street lights.

Suddenly, he felt a tingling sensation in the back of his neck and shoulders. He never knew where the sense came from, but he never questioned it. He stopped abruptly to pick up a rock and quickly glanced back the way he had just come. They hid themselves in the shadows but he had seen them.

Trouble. Two of them.

Following him. He turned down the next alley and reached into his coat. No Browning. He swore and picked up his pace. He glanced back again.

Four of them. Shit.

Somewhere in the distance he could hear music playing so he charged down the alley toward it, knocking over cans and boxes behind him to impede the progress of his pursuers. He looked back again. There was no mistake about it now.

There were four of them, and they were not hiding: they were coming after him.

He saw the glint of blades in their hands as they passed under a dim light at the other end of the alley. A fence appeared at his end of the alley. The music, which sounded very old-fashioned, seemed to be coming from somewhere on the other side of it. The fence was about six feet tall, but there were boxes and crates stacked against it.

One-armed hurdle? Not much of a chance.

He looked back again.

Not much of a choice.

He ran at the fence, jumped on one of the boxes, and grabbed the top rail of the fence in an effort to vault himself over. The fence had long since rotted at the foundation. It collapsed under Maletesta's weight. Luckily, he landed unhurt in a pile of rotten timber. He picked himself up and raced across the street. His four pursuers came to the fence as he entered the amusement park.

The amusement park was old, a pre-war relic of a lost venture by an American entrepreneur bent on bringing cotton candy entertainment around the world. The American hustler was long gone, but the park rolled on, wheezing and limping through its nineteenth century excitements.

The creaking Ferris wheel was missing lights, and several of the other mechanical rides were missing cars, carriages, and parts. A row of dirty tents which held the wonders of the freak show stood along the east side of the park. Arcade games and games of skill in which the customer didn't have a chance were lined up on the north side. Side by side in the middle of the park were the Tunnel of Love and the Octopus. The south side contained the rest of the rides and there seemed to be a concession selling something to eat or drink every 100 feet.

The park was three-quarters full and the people were enjoying themselves immensely.

Maletesta ducked into the first tent as his pursuers were crossing the street. It was a make-shift ladies' dressing room with clothes, shoes, and makeup scattered around a table and chairs. He peeked through flap in the tent wall which led to the performance area of the tent. The act was apparently over, and the audience was leaving noisily. A veiled woman left the stage and approached the flap. Maletesta stumbled backwards and fell over a chair. The woman entered.

She was wearing a shimmery light blue dress which was high at the knees and low at the shoulders. Brown eyes looked at Maletesta over the veil.

"Hello," purred the woman in an English accent, as Maletesta scrambled to his feet, "you are very welcome here."

Her eyes surveyed over him. "And quite handsome," she added.

Maletesta stood stupidly, not knowing what to say. As she glided toward him, she reached up to remove her veil. The veil fell away, revealing a full black beard.

"Excuse me," gulped Maletesta, plunging into the other room of the tent and leaving a shriek of wild laughter behind him.

The tent's barker yelled something at Maletesta when he emerged into the promenade between the two tents.

Maletesta smiled at him and dove back into the crowd, glancing around for his pursuers.

His plan to disappear in the crowd of revelers was foiled by being one of the few white men in the group. Most of them were Malays, Chinese, indigenous people from the interior and other islanders. He saw his pursuers as they saw him, several hundred feet behind him, pushing their way through the crowd. By now it was completely dark, except for the lights of the amusement park. He charged to the front of a line of people waiting to see the treasures of the next tent, pushing back the cursing ticket taker at the entry. Over the entrance, a faded sign proclaimed "Pretzel People--Beyond Belief!"

In the half light inside the tent, Maletesta saw writhing shapes preparing for their performance. A scene from *Dante's Inferno* flickered through his mind, the images coming back to him from the illustrations in one of his college text books. One of the shapes had his legs wrapped around his head, another had his arms twisted around his back and intertwined with his legs. There was squirming movement all over the stage as the contortionists got into position.

"Excuse me . . . excuse me," repeated Maletesta as he moved along, heading towards the back of the performance area. Some looked at him malevolently, while others stuck out

75

their tongues at him. An outsider. By now he heard a repeated call equivalent to "Hey Rube," the traditional carnival danger call, being shouted to all parts of the park in a variety of accents and pronunciations. The commotion he created at the entry to the tent delayed his original pursuers and the barkers. When he had pushed to the front of the line, everyone behind him rushed forward, inadvertently jamming his pursuers in the crowd and giving Maletesta a few minutes respite.

When he came out through the back of the tent, he crossed quickly to the shadow a large structure near the center of the park. He flattened himself against the wall and tried to control his rapid breathing. The crowd surged back and forth in front of him, enjoying the carnival.

Periodically, one of the carnival people passed, looking around for the troublemaker. Two of his pursuers passed more closely than he liked.

The other two are where?

He could not stay where he was. Sooner or later the park would close and he would be found. The calliope was playing "Take Me Out to the Ballgame," and Maletesta almost burst out laughing.

Well, I have to do something.

Maletesta began inching along the wall of the structure. No course of action came into mind, other than to get out of the park in one piece. His left shoulder continued to ache where he landed on it back at the fence. He moved to the right very slowly, his right arm out and against the wall. Suddenly, his fingers felt something.

A door jamb! Maletesta felt for where he hoped he'd find a door handle. His hopes fell when he couldn't find one. His hand moved rapidly over the door. The door opening was three feet from the ground.

Why? Who cares? Does it open? Ah, slot. A sliding door!

He pushed it tentatively to the right. It moved. He pushed it harder and got his shoulder into the opening and against the door. It opened wide enough for him to step in. He stepped in, landing in water up to his knees.

Hell, what now?

He closed the door behind him and waited for his eyes to adjust to the total darkness.

He felt movement in the water and heard some giggling. From up above somewhere he could hear a cranking sound. He could make out a crack of light in another wall about twenty five feet away.

Can't stand here all night.

Maletesta began sloshing through the water toward the faint light. Suddenly something bumped into him and he felt as if he jumped out of the water, splashing and turning toward the object at the same time.

A boat! What the Hell?

A man in the boat called out angrily into the dark, and Maletesta heard a woman giggling. The boat kept moving, pushed along by the steel shaft coming from overhead where the revolving machinery was located.

"Fixing," Maletesta called back, hoping they understood some English. "Fixing the motor . . .excuse me." He felt he could not say "excuse me" one more time that night.

It's a Tunnel of Love, for Christ's sake!

He reached the crack of light and his luck was holding.

Another door.

There was a step in the water and a narrow landing in front of the door. He climbed out of the water and went through the door, finding himself in a dimly lit stairway.

Must actually be a maintenance stairway.

He climbed up the stairs to a trap door and pushed it open.

Maletesta was in the engine room, clanking along, creating romantic journeys for lovers below. Maletesta sighed. He leaned against the wall and suddenly thought of Annemarie.

Annemarie.

He had refused to let her see him in the hospital. He wouldn't answer her letters.

Shouts from below aroused him from his reverie. He looked out one of the dirty windows and saw the four assassins down at the ticket booth for the Tunnel of Love. They were arguing with one of the carnival people. It became apparent that the carnival man would not let them into the structure, so two of them stood by the exit and two by the entrance. Another two husky carnival people went through the entrance. Any escape back through the way came was now effectively blocked.

If you can't go back, go forward, the captain always said. Sounds good; yeah, well, the problem is, he's dead. Didn't work for him. Well, I don't have any other options. Shit.

He pushed up the window and crawled out onto the roof. The roof was virtually flat with just enough slope to get rain into the gutters.

What now? Cannons to the right. Cannons to the left. Volleyed and thundered. Rode the Six Hundred. Into the jaws of death. Great. God, Gianni, think of something else! In Flanders fields where the poppies...Jesus!

He looked over to the other side of the building.

No. That'd be crazy. What are the odds?

Not far from the edge of the roof, an ancient Octopus ride was in motion, the carriages circling and rising and falling.

Can I do it? With one arm? No. Forget it.

Maletesta started back to the window of the engine room. When he neared the window, he heard them inside, talking loudly as they came confidently up the staircase, two carnival bouncers against a one-armed man.

Well, that settles it.

He stood up and watched the carriages of the Octopus for a minute, trying to time them. He ran down the roof as fast as he could in short distance, his legs taking huge strides.

At the gutter, he leaped, grabbing out with his arm at one of the carriages rising in its arc. He fell into the carriage as it almost reached the level of the roof. He held on tightly to the swivel at the top of the carriage.

Two children were in the carriage, laughing and clapping their hands at the show. Maletesta smiled at them weakly. He looked below and saw the Malays running toward the landing platform of the Octopus. People were crowding into the platform, pointing up at the rider on one of the carriages. One of the carnival workers stood poised at the brake, ready to stop the ride when Maletesta's carriage came down. Maletesta looked ahead, studying the arc of travel for the carriage. He saw that, as it descended, the carriage passed over an area where they fed the animals. Also, he could see one of the exits in the north side of the park.

Not much of a chance, but why not? So far, so good.

Maletesta leaped as soon as he was over the bales of hay and landed roughly in the middle of them. He was rolling as he hit, using his arm to propel himself off the bales on to the ground. He glanced back quickly and saw his four pursuers breaking out of the crowd and running toward him.

He ran past a tilt-a-floor and a hall of mirrors. Next to the mirrors was a revolving barrel, a carnival staple which was a challenge to walking sideways without falling down. When he was a kid, it was his favorite in the Fun House at Playland at the Beach. He bested his friends every time. He slowed down slightly and glanced back at the assassins. They were closing in on him. The lead man had taken a kris out of his sleeve and he saw the blade glint in the overhead lights. The barrel was revolving slowly, but there was no one in it.

Maletesta waited until the last possible moment, raised the middle finger of his right hand at them, and plunged into the barrel. He executed a perfect running side step, traversing the barrel in a matter of seconds.

The assassins, closing in for the kill, came charging in after him, unaware of how the barrel worked. They were soon in a jumble, tumbling and yelling, losing their knives and unable to regain their footing. Maletesta ran chuckling through the park exit and out into the safety of the dark streets.

ELEVEN

Sibu

The breakfast plates were being cleared away by the waiter as Hombardt, Willis, and Maletesta sat with their coffee. Maletesta's plate was virtually untouched. He had no appetite, which was providential for Willis who had eaten his own breakfast, all the rolls on the plate in the center of the table, and Maletesta's scrambled eggs. The dining room of the Empire was nearly empty. There were two Chinese businessmen at a table across the room. Another waiter hovered near the door to the kitchen.

The ceiling fans revolved slowly and silently. There was a faint smell of furniture polish and mahogany wainscoting shone in the morning sunlight beaming in through the French windows on the south side of the room. Tables with crisp white linen and empty chairs awaited customers. Trade and tourism were still not back to pre-war levels. Willis belched contentedly and Hombardt added sugar to his coffee while Maletesta jabbed at the air with his spoon, punctuating his points.

"Doctor Hombardt," he exclaimed, "this expedition has started off with a lot of unanswered questions. Something stinks. Something is wrong here! Why did the pirates come down to the passengers' cabins first? They usually take over the ship first. What really happened to old Van Vliet? Why did Van Vliet try to cut me out of the expedition? Why was I followed and attacked last night? There's far too many questions for coincidence!"

Maletesta set the spoon down on the table. "I say that the least we should do is get a new guide. Something's not quite copasetic about Van Vliet."

Hombardt stirred his coffee. Then he slowly stuffed his pipe with the special mixture he had brought with him, lit it, and looked at Maletesta and back to his pipe several times before he spoke.

"Mister Maletesta," he began in the tone of one who is still in a lecture room, you teach English literature. It goes without saying that literature is a highly imaginative field. I believe that you are letting your imagination run away with you."

"Letting my…" Maletesta interrupted.

"Allow me to finish, Mister Maletesta! I listened politely to your wild accusations. Now, I shall answer them."

Hombardt held up one finger.

"One, pirate attacks in the Celebes Sea are not uncommon events."

"Scary, though," Willis chimed with a shudder.

He held up two fingers.

"Two, there is no evidence to suggest anything untoward happened to the elder Van Vliet or that the younger Van Vliet is not a competent guide."

He held up three fingers.

"And, three, when you venture into the neighborhoods of the lower classes in any country after dark, you are inviting trouble upon yourself."

Willis nodded and belched again. It was only nine o'clock, but already perspiration glowed on his forehead and his shirt was growing damp. He turned to Maletesta.

"John," he said to Maletesta, "I think you worry too much. We are going to have a wonderful expedition and it will be a great success! You'll see!"

"I just can't convince you, can I?" Maletesta replied, looking from one to the other. He slumped in his chair. "You're going through with it."

"I've already sent a wire to Sister Agatha," said Hombardt. "Tomorrow we'll be on our way. Think of it, man!" Hombardt's eyes were aglow. "A major discovery at our finger tips! The world at our feet!"

Hombardt could barely contain himself. He poured pepper out on the table and pushed it around to represent the river. The salt cellar became Sibu; the creamer and upended coffee cups which he cleaned with his napkin became the volcano and the mountains where the limestone caves were. He laid spoons and knives on end where the river was. He traced over the journey with his finger. Hombardt's eyes glowed as he detailed the mission ahead of them and its consequences. Willis sat transfixed. Four days up the river. Three days to the mountains and the caves. The setup of the equipment. The dig. The records. The find. The first man. Returning in triumph to the States. History was being made by the three people at this table.

In spite of his reservations, Maletesta found himself being drawn into the spell cast by Hombardt.

Maybe I am worrying too much. Maybe there are coincidences. Am I being over-anxious? Can I trust my gut feelings anymore? I still have the dreams. Maybe the dreams have taken over my imagination and my new reality, whatever that is. Maybe...maybe...

Hombardt pushed himself away from the mess he's made on the table and stood up.

"So I suggest we have a relaxing day and a good night's sleep. We meet here at 7 o'clock sharp for a quick breakfast and await Van Vliet's driver. Cheerio!"

The class was over. Hombardt marched out of the dining room, trailing smoke and Willis.

Maletesta walked out onto the hotel veranda and finished his cigarette. Doubts began to fill his mind again when he was away from the aura of Hombardt's easy confidence. He turned over the events of the last two weeks. Sister Agatha interviewing him about the expedition, about Peking Man . . . Peking Man! He had forgotten. Someone had supposedly seen something on a ship in Sibu.

Yes, a prisoner saw the crates. What a long shot! If Hombardt thinks I'm imaginative, what in the world would he think of Sister Agatha? No wonder she didn't tell him. Not much scientific evidence. Regardless, I told her I'd do some checking, fool's errand or not. There must be a record of shipping somewhere.

Maletesta woke up one of the rickshaw drivers who was sleeping against the railing of the veranda and asked the driver to take him to the building of records.

The clerk at Government House was extremely polite and extremely helpful. He made sounds of regret as he checked through file cabinets and clip boards and reshuffled papers.

Maletesta waited at the counter. The clerk returned.

"I'm very sorry, sir, but many records of shipping and arrivals and departures during the occupation have been lost. What is decidedly odd in this case is that the first two months of 1942 have disappeared. I don't understand it."

"Why is it odd?" Maletesta asked.

The clerk made a face.

"Usually," he began, "there are a few days missing here; a few days there. This is very unusual. I just don't understand it. Of course, I wasn't here at the time. I was with His Majesty's forces in Burma."

"Who was here during the occupation?"

"Virtually impossible to say. The collaborators were killed by the locals at the end of the war. I'm told that the Japanese changed the staff frequently because they were suspicious of spies. I'm very sorry."

"Were any records kept anywhere else?" Maletesta tried to hide the disappointment in his voice. This was the only lead that he could think of.

"No sir. I'm very sorry," the clerk repeated.

"Thank you for your time."

"No trouble at all. Good day."

Maletesta turned and began walking across the marble lobby to the street.

"Excuse me, sir!" the clerk called suddenly.

"Yes?" Maletesta replied, turning back.

"I just recalled something which may be helpful to you. There was a junior clerk--very junior I might add—who worked here at that time and who still lives in town."

"Where can I find him?"

"I believe he's been seen around the Shining Light Mission. I think he sleeps there in return for sweeping the place."

"Where is it and what's his name?"

"Down on the waterfront about a quarter mile from the customs office on the same side of the street. His name is Javier. Javier Le Boo…"

"Le Boo?"

"Le Boo. He didn't know his parents. Picked his own surname, as it were."

"Thanks very much," Maletesta said and retraced his steps out of the building.

Ten minutes later he stood outside the Shining Light mission. It was a small dilapidated building sandwiched between two run down warehouses. The sign on the window said "Shining Light" in faded painted letters and underneath "God Remembrs" in peeling paper letters. Maletesta could not see into the dirty windows and the door between them was locked.

Maletesta knocked on the door and waited. No response. He knocked again and called. He heard some scraping noises inside. He waited. The noise had stopped but the door remained closed.

He knocked again and called louder.

There was a rattle of a bolt from within and the door slowly opened. A disheveled old man peered out, squinting at the sunlight.

"I thought you gone," the man said. "Shining Light closed," he mumbled, looking everywhere except at Maletesta. Then he looked straight at him as a thought came into his mind.

"You got any money?" the man asked. "Very poor people here."

Maletesta looked into the bleary old harmless eyes. He saw his Uncle Johnny, his namesake, the family drunk. Hardly anyone ever talked about Uncle Johnny except when his father would say he was a good machinist when he wanted to be. Uncle Johnny never got invited around, but young John and his cousins loved it when he suddenly showed up at a holiday dinner. He was always more fun than the other adults, down on the floor with the kids, his pockets full of rock candy, his breath smelling of peppermint.

"Yeah," Maletesta answered, "I've got money, but first I want to talk. Are you Mister Le Boo?"

"Sure, Le Boo. Mister? Ha ha! Talk whatever you want. Come inna my office," Le Boo laughed, displaying a perfect set of teeth which seemed out of place in the alcohol-ravaged face.

They entered the mission, which was a long narrow room, worn but clean, with rows of folding chairs facing a podium and a table in front of the room. Le Boo directed Maletesta to a chair at a table and took one opposite him.

"You wanna be saved, brudda?" Le Boo asked. "Get Jesus? The reverend be here at 4 o'clock."

"That's OK. I came to see you, not the reverend. I want to talk about when you worked at Government House. Do you remember?"

"Government House? Don't like Le Boo up there! They say Le Boo lazy, Le Boo do things wrong . . ."

Maletesta held up his hand to interrupt the litany.

"Wait a minute, Mister Le Boo! Wait a minute. I mean when the Japanese were here. Can you remember?"

"Japanese." Le Boo spit on the floor. "They make fun of Le Boo. Hold bottle out. 'Dance, Boo, dance.'" He spit on the floor again.

"Right after the war started," Maletesta began, "a ship came here with prisoners. Do you remember it?"

"Le Boo remember many things. Many ships. Some with guns, some with prisoners, some with soldiers. Many soldiers. Many killing."

He frowned and his eyes began to glaze over. Suddenly he was alert again.

"What you want? Get Jesus? Reverend here at 4 o'clock."

"No. No reverend. Just you."

Maletesta took a deep breath and hoped the interview wasn't slipping away from him. "One ship. With prisoners and a special cargo. Very secret. Secret."

Carefully holding his index finger to his lips, Maletesta leaned closer to Le Boo, who seemed to be concentrating.

"January or February of 1942. Four years ago. Do you remember it?" he asked softly.

"Sure. Japanese." Le Boo spit on the floor again. Then he looked at the spittle. "Better clean before reverend come. Four o'clock."

"Le Boo!" Maletesta shouted. "One ship! Secret cargo! Prisoners! Big secret! Remember? Big secret!"

Le Boo recoiled from the loud voice, and then he began speaking slowly.

"Yes. Remember. Secret boxes. Prisoners carry to warehouse with bombs, bullets."

Le Boo began rubbing his hands together slowly, studying his palms, his knuckles, his nails.

"Le Boo see. Japanese soldiers not worry. Le Boo drunk. Ha ha. They laugh. Shoot prisoners...no! no! Shoot prisoners, shoot."

Le Boo slumped over and lay his head on the table.

Maletesta waited for almost a full minute.

"What is it?" he finally asked quietly.

"Hurt Le Boo. Soldiers hurt Le Boo. Get Jesus."

"What happened to the cargo, Mister Le Boo?" Maletesta whispered slowly.

"Upriver. They take upriver with bombs and bullets."

"Thank you, Mister Le Boo." Maletesta laid some paper money on the table and rose. "This is for you, Mister Le Boo, not the mission."

"Get Jesus," the old man said.

TWELVE

Sibu

"Have you ever been to Europe, Willis?" Hombardt asked.

"No, I've never had that pleasure, Doctor Hombardt."

"Pity. Some day you should, you know. Won't be quite like it was before the war, but, then again, nothing is."

The two of them were walking along the docks of the Rajang river watching Van Vliet's men load the equipment and provisions onto flat-bottomed boats which were powered by outboard motors. The boats were a variation of the indigenous gobong, a slim dugout-like vessel with a detachable roof. Van Vliet's hired boats were slightly wider, so they could carry more goods up and down the river. The boats were also equipped with long poles which were used when the river was too shallow or full of vegetation for the outboard motors.

Van Vliet and Kwan were everywhere: giving directions to laborers, stowing equipment, meticulously supervising the beginning of the expedition. Hombardt was obviously pleased by the show of efficiency. He elected to carry the swagger stick and banged it on his thigh as he walked along.

"They remind me of the punts on the Thames," he said, "of course, there were no motors, humph, just undergraduates and oars. I spent a year there, studying under Gardner."

Willis nodded, unsure of what answer should be given.

"A grand England, that." Hombardt continued. "I wonder what changes we shall see in this new order of nations. All these two-penny countries clamoring for their opinion to be heard."

He pointed toward two of the laborers nearby.

"These beggars probably think they should be in charge. Can you imagine what a mess the world would be if they were in charge?"

"Problem with Communists, sir," Willis added, finding a place to make his contribution to the conversation.

"Exactly right, Willis, exactly right. Fill their fuzzy heads with fuzzy ideas, then what do you have, eh? The end of civilization, Willis, that's what we'll have!"

"Terrible, just terrible," Willis clucked.

"The Russians are not far behind us in this business, Willis," Hombardt whispered conspiratorially. "I've heard stories about their interest in the Yeti, the so-called Abominable Snowman. They think, that--if he exists—he might be part of this chain of descent. I wouldn't be surprised to hear about them in this area some day. It would be very bad for America if the Russians found our man before we did!"

The two of them continued their discussion along the dock.

Maletesta was dressed in army fatigues with the Browning in place under a light field jacket. He watched the proceedings with interest as he sat on a rusty hand truck under the overhang of one of the warehouses. It seemed to him that the crew who were loading the six boats were presumably the porters who would carry the whole kit into the mountains. They did not seem to know Van Vliet or Kwan. They were small, strong men who seemed clumsy around the boats. They handled the cargo easily but responded to commands sluggishly and did not go about their business like experienced boatmen. He wondered about it for a while and then put it out of his mind.

Last night his flashbacks had replayed themselves again. The usual images of the non-com with his sword, his arm on the ground, Lonnie firing--but this time new images forced their way into his nightmare world: pirates, carnival freaks, spinning, spinning, suddenly the specter of Javier Le Boo. Le Boo: the weak link in a weak lead.

Sister Agatha had to be kidding. If Lee Boo could be believed, if the whole thing wasn't an alcoholic pipe dream;

*then the missing fossils of Peking Man had gone up this same
river four years ago. Where? To what? The monkeys? The
snakes? Perhaps one of the aboriginal tribes studying
anthropology?*

"Impossible!" Maletesta snorted aloud.

*Most likely, the bones are at the bottom of the sea in the
hold of a torpedoed ship. Or dumped in the garbage
somewhere in China. Dem bones, dem bones, dem dry bones;
dem bones, dem . . . get serious, Gianni! Poor old drunk'll tell
you anything for a couple of bucks or a chance to sleep
indoors. Where did Uncle Johnny go when he wasn't visiting? I
never knew. I never wondered.*

He dropped the end of his cigarette and squashed it out
with his boot. He might have been killing a snake for all the
strength he put into extinguishing the cigarette.

*This whole thing stinks. Look at those two clowns parading
on the docks. Where did Sister Agatha ever find them? And Van
Vliet and Kwan, like somebody out of a movie. When will
Wallace Beery show up? I should have stayed home. To hell
with it and to hell with these guys.*

Maletesta sauntered down to the docks.

"Well, Jungle Jim, which one's mine?" he asked Van Vliet,
indicating the boats.

"You Yanks, great kidders, aren't you?" Van Vliet replied.

"Sometimes." Maletesta's mood was heavy.

Hombardt and Willis appeared.

"Doctor Hombardt and I will be in the lead boat," Van
Vliet announced, "Willis and Kwan in the third, and you in the
fifth."

"Why don't we use bigger boats? We wouldn't need so
many," Maletesta asked.

"The bigger boats can't handle the shallow waters upriver,"
Van Vliet answered, smiling slightly.

Maletesta kicked at a rotten spot in the bow of the boat nearest him.

"These are a lot cheaper, too," he scowled.

"They appear to be perfectly serviceable!" interjected Hombardt, who had come up behind while they were talking.

Maletesta laughed derisively.

"Since when did you become a sailor, Doctor?" he snarled.

There was a clamor of angry voices, Hombardt, Willis, and Van Vliet. Finally, Hombardt's voice prevailed.

"Frankly, Mister Maletesta, I find your attitude completely reprehensible! You have been nasty, suspicious, and uncooperative since this expedition began. If it wasn't for Sister Agatha, I'd order you off this expedition!"

Hombardt fumed and waved his swagger stick.

Maletesta winced.

"Order me? You're going to order me? Now you're General Hombardt, and you're going to order me?"

He glared at Hombardt and Willis, standing next to Van Vliet and Kwan. He saw their faces and their hatred clearly. Then the faces began to fade and shimmer. He didn't understand what they were saying; his head was pounding inside; there was a roaring noise in his ears.

What are they saying? Kill the bastards! Now!

Maletesta's right hand was clenching and unclenching. He felt the weight of the Browning inside his jacket, two seconds away. The roaring continued in his head. *Kill the bastards, Gianni! Now!*

Suddenly, he blinked and held his eyes shut for a moment. He gained control of himself. The episode has passed.

What's wrong with me? I'm ready to kill them.

He turned abruptly and walked down to the fifth boat. One of the boatmen steadied the boat as he stepped in and took a seat midship. He looked back at the others still watching him.

"Well, are we going or not?" he said and pulled his field cap down over his eyes.

While Hombardt and Willis were boarding their respective boats, Van Vliet leaned down to Kwan's ear.

"I told you, you should have killed him the other night."

"Don't worry, boss, there's still plenty of time."

Kwan tapped the parang he wore at his side. Then he turned to the boatmen and shouted out orders in their language. One by one the flatboats left the docks and began chugging upriver into the largely uncharted interior of Borneo.

THIRTEEN

Borneo

"What a place! Is it like this in the highlands, too?" Willis asked, as he splashed the 6-12 mosquito repellent into his hands and slapped it on his neck. A continual hum of insects, most of them unseen, filled the air.

Willis was perched on a camp stool outside his tent and looked extremely uncomfortable in the light of the Coleman lantern.

"No, thank God, from what they've told me," Hombardt answered from his nearby stool, encased in a cloud of pipe smoke.

"You should take up smoking, Willis. Calms the mind . . . and creates a smudge pot," Hombardt chuckled. He exhaled more smoke, and went back to reading his bound edition of *Moby Dick*.

Willis put the repellent on the folding camp table between them and continued writing in the journal on his lap.

June 3, 1946. This is our fourth day out of Sibu. I did not have enough energy to write yesterday. The heat was too oppressive. We are many miles upriver. The river has gotten more narrow, and the trees have closed over our heads. Actually, it's becoming quite beautiful if you like the jungle surroundings.

The trees overhead are like a lattice work, lacing in and out of each other. Sometimes you can see patches of the sky and then you won't for several hours. There seem to be many birds and animals flying and jumping between the branches. I've tried to imitate some of the whistles of the birds, but they are so varied, impossible.

There are more flying insects than I have ever seen and the nonstop buzzing would drive you crazy if you don't just ignore it. Each day grows more humid and sticky and it feels like the walls of the jungle are closing in on us.

The walls are vines and creepers tangled in trees and roots. The ground can be very mossy and full of decaying leaves and plants because the sun never shines on it, or only for a very short time. Yesterday morning was quite stunning, waking up to a fog around us and then seeing the sunlight filter down through the canopy of trees overhead. Some trees have roots above the waterline of the river! We have had a lot of rain, but it doesn't always reach us. We can hear it on the high trees, but the leaves and branches are so dense very little direct rain comes down on us.

If I could bring anything back home with me, it would have to be some of the plants. They are spectacular! Their colors are absolutely beautiful, shades of red, orange, purple, yellow. And another amazing thing: some plants grow on other ones! And in tree branches! I don't know what their names are, or if they even have any names! We might be the first white men who have ever seen them!

We've also seen quite a few crocodiles (or alligators, I'm not sure which--ugly beasts all the same) and many different kinds of birds. Monkeys have also been watching us from the trees and chattering. It's like a Tarzan movie, but it's real. Van Vliet shot two of the monkeys, and our natives retrieved them and ate them the night before last for dinner. I didn't have any . . . Willis stopped and swatted at the air. He let out a sigh of resignation and began again. *Late yesterday afternoon we stopped at a native longhouse. It was primitive but quite clever. They build their houses out of bamboo and rattan and several feet off the ground to keep out snakes and leeches (my goodness!) We had to climb up a ladder which was a log with notches cut into it.*

Van Vliet told us that the people in this house are called the Iban, which is one of the largest tribes on Borneo. They were quite friendly, although I noticed some gruesome old heads hanging from the ceiling beams. Van Vliet assured us that no one had done any head hunting in years.

The hunters of the family came back while we were there, so this apparently called for a celebration. They appear to be a very simple people and like to celebrate just about anything it seems. The hunters came back with their dogs, and the dogs stayed under the house making quite a racket fighting over their food. The hunters were dripping wet, having just washed in the river.

It was dark inside the house with the main light coming from the cooking fire. We had to sit on the floor with everyone else, which I found to be uncomfortable. (My knees never seem to bend the right way!) However, I was able to wedge my back against one of the corner poles so it wasn't too bad, but my foot kept going to sleep. There was a lot of laughter, continual talking, and exclamations while, according to our translator Kwan, the hunters told their story about the hunt. Someone banged gongs at various points during the story. I guess it's quite an event for primitive people.

We were given a drink made out of rice which was somehow distilled to make it very powerful. I got a headache from the first cup and the second one made me dizzy.

Thereafter, I sipped it slowly and, when no one was looking, tipped it out into a crack in the floor.

Our dinner of rice and wild pig was actually quite tasty, which surprised me. I must say though that it was difficult to concentrate on eating with all the movement around us, people talking, carrying on, and dancing.

The Iban are very dark and have straight black hair. By the light of the fire, their teeth and the whites of their eyes shine like stars. Every so often one of them would come up and grab me, laughing. Some of the women wore only a skirt-like thing leaving their bosoms exposed while others wore tops. I wasn't sure where to look!

Van Vliet told me that almost all the clothing was made by the tribe out of material from the forest and the jungle, but I noticed one or two army surplus shirts. The men wore loin cloths generally and had those damned ever-present long bush knives hanging from their waist. Some had hair hanging from the handles and Van Vliet said that the hair was from dead enemies, but I think he was just trying to put a scare into the tourists (ha ha).

John Maletesta remarked that he thought the younger women were quite pretty, but Doctor Hombardt and I agreed that, after all, they're really just savages, not much more developed that the people whose fossils we were looking for. It's hard for me to see them as "pretty."

The longhouse got so noisy that Doctor Hombardt and I went back to our tents shortly after dinner. Van Vliet, Maletesta and Kwan stayed later. This morning they told us about the wildness of the dancing, but neither Doctor Hombardt nor I were really interested.

John Maletesta has loosened up quite a bit and is not so defensive. He seems to have relaxed a bit since we've come into the jungle. He's definitely not as testy as he was in Sibu. He tries to talk with our natives and seems to enjoy studying all the different kinds of plants we see. He's been very cordial for the last three or four days, which has been pleasantly surprising. (He was insufferable on the ship and in Sibu!)

I still don't understand why Sister Agatha insisted that he come along. She talked about him as a kind of bodyguard, but there are really no problems in the jungle, as long as you watch where you're going. John's very awkward with one arm and all and gets pretty banged up when he slips. We've all had our falls around camp, due to the unevenness of the slippery ground--

I think the old nun just wanted to give him something to do.

Speaking of slippery, it rained again today and, because of the openings in the trees above, we got quite wet. We are continually fighting the rain, the humidity, or the moistness.

As a consequence, everything that is not covered tightly with waterproofed material, is either wet or damp. When I finish this entry, I must return the journal and my pen to its waterproof pouch.

As Willis continued his writing, Maletesta sat outside his tent. The night's encampment was made in an area cleared that afternoon by Van Vliet's crew. Three tents were set up: Van Vliet and Kwan in one, Hombardt and Willis in the second, and Maletesta in the remaining tent.

The boatmen and porters slept under the removable boat canopies which were used as shelter on land and then re-affixed to the gunwales of the boats on the following morning. There were lanterns at each tent and a fire in the middle of the encampment.

Maletesta did not light his lantern. He was listening, watching. He heard the creatures in the jungle and their struggle for survival. A screech, a rustle, and then silence.

The hunters and the hunted. Isn't that what we all are? Which am I? A teacher? Probably a hunted. A crippled teacher planning to rust away in a small college. Every student glances at my empty sleeve and then looks away quickly. It would have been better if I died. Right there in battle, bringing that bastard down with me. A corpsman saved my life. Thanks a lot. Now I can be another Pete Gray, the only one-armed major league outfielder in the history of baseball. Problem is, the major leaguers with two arms back from the war and the Pete Grays have been sent home. Maybe I'll die here, in battle. That's it. Like with the pirates. I didn't do too badly. Got the best of those bastards at the carnival too. Never thought all those days fooling around at Playland would save my life. Laughing Sal to the rescue!

He smiled at the thought, lit another cigarette and glanced over at the other tents.

Van Vliet and Kwan had turned out their lantern and retired. Hombardt was still reading and Willis was locked in concentration on his journal, scribbling away. Encircling Willis' boot was a snake about four feet long.

Maletesta froze. Then he quietly pulled the Browning out of his shoulder holster and slipped the safety off.

"Willis," he whispered, "don't move an inch. There's a snake on your boot."

Something in Maletesta's voice prompted Willis to obey without question. His pen stopped and he gulped. Hombardt looked up and blinked. The snake slithered upward toward Willis' thigh. Green and black shimmered in the light of the gas lantern. Maletesta could see its tongue darting in and out.

Maletesta had crossed his right leg over his left as he called to Willis. He rested his forearm on his right knee, straightening his arm out and sighting the place behind Willis' calf where the snake's head would next appear as it made its way up Willis' leg. He took up the slack on the trigger and waited. Sweat poured down Willis' face as he held himself as still as he could. Maletesta could hear the hiss of the Coleman. He kept his breathing steady, his eyes focused over the sights.

The snake stopped momentarily at something it sensed on the leg of the camp stool and then continued on its climb. Its head cleared Willis' calf.

Maletesta squeezed and fired. Willis jumped and screamed, knocking over his chair and the camp table.

There was pandemonium in the encampment, matched by the sudden silence in the jungle. The boatmen and porters rolled out of their bedding and drew their weapons. Van Vliet came rushing out of his tent with a Mannlicher rifle in his hands, followed by Kwan brandishing his parang.

"What the hell...what's going on?" Van Vliet yelled, quickly looking all around and finally seeing the pistol in Maletesta's hand.

Hombardt alone had remained seated.

"A remarkable shot," he said blandly. "I've heard about that sort of thing and always thought it was the product of over-active imaginations." He paused and pointed to something on the ground near the corner of the tent flap. "There it is: what's left of the head."

"Pit viper," Van Vliet intoned, turning to Willis. "You're lucky, mate."

By now, Willis, who was shivering uncontrollably, had shaken the rest of the snake's body off his leg. They all stood looking at the dead snake and at Maletesta. The boat men and porters spoke among themselves, pointing at the snake and at Maletesta.

"Quite a shot, Mister Maletesta," Van Vliet said, "do you do that often?"

"Surprised myself," Maletesta said, thumbing the safety back on and slipping the automatic pistol back into its holster. "Let's all go to bed before I have to try it again."

Howard'll never believe this. Not bad, Gianni. Snake's head wasn't more than an inch and a half wide.

The table was set upright again and Willis picked up his journal and pen from where they had fallen. Still quivering slightly, he held his hand out to Maletesta.

"Thank you, John," he said as he shook Maletesta's hand. Then he went into his tent.

Hombardt emptied out his pipe as the others returned to their shelters.

"Very impressive demonstration, Maletesta," he said and indicated Willis' unoccupied stool with his pipe. "Did you develop that skill in the service?"

"No," Maletesta answered as he sat down, "the Army fine-tuned it for me, but I had done a lot of shooting before then...and playing baseball."

"Playing baseball? How does that apply?"

"There's an amount of hand-to-eye coordination in all sports. You look, you throw. You watch, you catch. In shooting, you look, you shoot. They shoot...you duck."

They both laughed easily.

"Do you know how old I am, Maletesta?" Hombardt asked abruptly.

"Uh...forty-five?"

"Fifty-eight. I stay fit and most people think I'm younger. Not that it matters. The clock and the calendar don't care how fit I am. They know I'm fifty-eight."

Hombardt twisted on the camp stool uncomfortably.

"Can you understand how important this expedition is to me?" he asked, looking directly into Maletesta's eyes.

"I think so."

Hombardt paused and grimaced.

"No. I don't think you can," he said. "You're too young. You have a whole life ahead of you." His mood had changed again. He stood up and walked toward the tent.

"Good night, Maletesta," he said and disappeared into the tent.

"Good night, Doctor Hombardt," Maletesta replied. He turned off the Coleman and went back to his own tent.

FOURTEEN

Borneo

The next morning began uneventfully. After a quick breakfast of surplus military rations, the expedition broke camp and once again took to the river.

Van Vliet selected this river which flowed into the Rajang for two reasons: it led to the mountain destination of the expedition and a smaller river paralleled it to the clearing where he planned to make camp tonight. He thought briefly about Maletesta. Last night's incident once again demonstrated what a dangerous adversary he was. Maletesta was a nagging problem, but that would be solved soon. The rest was easy.

Toward midday, the expedition came upon a slow moving section of the river with a buildup of creepers and water plants. The outboard motors were shut down and the poles were brought out. The going was slow and laborious and as Maletesta watched the process, he remembered pictures of Mississippi River boatmen he had seen in a history book. He noticed once again that the crew members did not seem to be experienced boatmen. They handled the poles awkwardly.

Why? Why don't they know what they're doing? A professional guide like Van Vliet shouldn't have a crew who handled boats clumsily. Also, they would know each other. There would be camaraderie with Van Vliet, like a platoon. My platoon. Lonnie, Daly, Felipe, Higgins, the rest--thought like a team, moved like a team...

"Look, over there, in those trees! Do you see it?"

It was Willis, yelling and pointing toward a dense stand of banyan trees about thirty yards from the bank on the starboard side of the boat. In his excitement, he almost scuttled the boat he was in. His boatmen steadied it with some judicious pole work.

"The Wild Man of Borneo! An orangutan! Can you see it in the branches?"

Beyond the bank was a small clearing created by animals grazing, presumably elephants. The elephants were no longer there, but swinging in the limbs of a banyan at the edge of the clearing was a large orangutan, red haired and easily two hundred pounds. Periodically he watched the boaters, then swung gracefully to adjoining trees and back.

Following Van Vliet's orders, the expedition temporarily moored their crafts by the boatmen sculling to exposed roots in the bank and holding the boats to them. The air was alive with the chattering of unseen monkeys, the calls of birds, and the ever-present hum of flying insects. The crew watched the antics of the orangutan with glee. Willis pulled a camera out of his back pack, anchored himself with one foot on a large root and began taking pictures of the orangutan. Even Hombardt smiled slightly.

The mood was shattered when Van Vliet unlimbered his Mannlicher and snapped off a shot. The shot went high and split a limb above the animal's head. The orangutan looked up at the broken branch. Van Vliet worked the bolt of his rifle. The empty case went spinning into the river and a fresh cartridge driven home.

"Stop, you fool!" Maletesta yelled.

"What, a sentimentalist?" Van Vliet snickered, lowering his rifle slightly. "After all this shooting you've been doing, especially what I heard about on the Star of Malaya?" He twitched as he spoke.

"That ape isn't bothering anybody! Put that damn rifle down!"

The orangutan continued to swing in the trees, oblivious of the debate going on about him. Van Vliet turned halfway toward Maletesta, the rifle swinging in his direction. Maletesta steadied himself in his boat which was rocking gently against the bank. The Browning was within easy reach, cocked and locked in his shoulder holster.

A quick grab, roll toward the bank.

The movement of Van Vliet's rifle stopped. They watched each other.

"That's quite enough, Mister Maletesta!" Hombardt commanded. "Mister Van Vliet is our guide for this expedition and therefore responsible for the success of it. He can do whatever he likes, as long as it does not jeopardize this expedition! We don't need any unnecessary heroics! After all, it's only an animal."

Maletesta's eyes glazed over for seconds and then returned to focus. He took a breath and then lowered his head.

"All right," he said, shortly. "Let's go."

"Good," Hombardt said. He exhaled and nodded to his boatman. The boatman began pushing away from the bank. Van Vliet remained standing as they pulled away. At midstream, Van Vliet twisted quickly and fired back at the trees. The orangutan fell, crashing through the lower branches before it hit the ground. Van Vliet looked at Maletesta and smiled. Maletesta's jaw tightened. Hombardt stared straight ahead.

Before they started out that morning, Van Vliet had told the party that they would make camp that night at a spot he knew on this river which was not far from where they would change rivers again for the final voyage to the foothills of the highlands. Hombardt was pleased to hear that only two days remained on the river, followed by a two day trek to the caves. He was eager to set up the dig.

The expedition reached the designated area shortly before sundown. It was a wide expanse of land created by the vagaries of nature, a clearing in the jungle. In another few years, the clearing would no longer exist, having been reclaimed by the jungle. The boats were pulled up on the river bank, and the porters began setting up the encampment, unrolling the tents and hammering the pegs into the ground. The cooks started a fire and began sorting through their stores for the evening meal. There was an air of tiredness about the encampment, including the boatmen and porters, due to the long day's journey upriver and the never-ending struggle against the humidity and the insects.

Maletesta went back to his boat to retrieve a bottle of insect repellent. Hombardt stood in the middle of the clearing studying the workers, and Willis unfolded a camp stool, sat down and opened his journal. Unnoticed by anyone, Van Vliet and Kwan slipped silently out of the clearing and into the jungle.

Willis slapped at his neck when the dart hit him. He grabbed it and looked at it and began shrieking. Then he fell and kicked a little. Then he was dead.

Hombardt witnessed it and stood dumfounded as darts flew by him. Some of the porters fell, and the rest of the men had hardly drawn their weapons when a howling mob burst out of the jungle on three sides of the clearing. Hombardt was speared in the back. The porters and boatmen were no match for the surprise and the ferocity of the attack. Parangs, swords and spears were being wielded viciously by the attackers. The boat crews of the expedition tried to flee but were met by more attackers. The clearing rang with the screams of frightened and dying men.

At the first sound of alarm, Maletesta ran back to the camp, his pistol in his hand. He shot two of the attackers. He saw Hombardt and Willis lying dead on the ground.

Where is Van Vliet?

He turned just barely in time to fire at one of the attackers who had come up behind him.

He took a glancing blow off his forehead from a war club. The clearing was spinning in front of him as he staggered backward, firing the Browning as fast as he could. He wasn't sure if he was hitting anyone, but many of the attackers had dropped to the ground under the fusillade.

He ejected an empty clip, grabbed the pistol in his left armpit, inserted a fresh magazine, and fired again and again.

Get out, Gianni! Get out! Get away! Can't help anybody. They're dead. Where's Van Vliet? Look out! OK, got him. That guy looks like one of the pirates. Gold teeth! What the hell? Got him. What the hell's in my eyes? Blood? Empty again, damn it, get to cover!

Maletesta plunged deeper into the jungle, with blood running down his face from the head wound. The attackers were reticent to follow and run into that burst of fire.

When the cries of the dying ended, Van Vliet and Kwan reappeared in the clearing.

"Take heads," Van Vliet ordered, "loot the bodies but leave them where they are. We'll notify the authorities when we get back, and they'll send someone out to check."

Van Vliet stepped quickly through the encampment checking each body as the gang of attackers began their grisly task with their parangs. Suddenly, he stopped and looked back over the dead.

"Maletesta! Where's Maletesta? Maletesta!" he suddenly shouted, grabbing the man closest to him and yelling into his face.

"Where's the one-armed man?"

The man pointed to the edge of the clearing and at several other dead members of the ambush party.

"Bang, bang, bang, bang," he said, backing up and making his fingers like a pistol.

"Sod it! Go after him, you cowards!" Van Vliet screamed. He shouldered his rifle and fired wildly into the jungle. Kwan came up beside him.

"Don't worry, boss," he said, grinning, "he won't live in jungle. Be dead tomorrow."

Nonetheless, for a few moments the two of them stared at the jungle, wondering.

FIFTEEN

Burlingame, California

"I'm not gettin' your meanin', Aggie."

Con Buckley cocked his head like an Airedale and squinted across the table at Sister Agatha. It was an idiosyncratic habit he had developed over the years during dockside debates and conversations and was probably a result of being able to hear better out of his right ear than his left. An adversary once suggested that it had come about from living too long with dogs, and he received a black eye for his analysis.

Buckley was past fifty. A fringe of salt and pepper hair stuck out from under his traditional white longshore cap and deep wrinkles permeated his face. He was not very tall and he stood with a slight stoop from years of unloading cargo in dank holds of ships on West Coast docks. But he was still tough. The young Mission hoodlums known as the White Shoe Boys stepped out of his way as he approached with his rolling gait. People often mistook him for a seaman.

"No," he'd state proudly in the remains of a Munster brogue, "Not a seaman, I worked 'longshore with Harry." Then, to anyone who would listen, he'd recount in full detail the epic battle of Rincon Hill between the police and Harry Bridges' fledgling longshoremen's union during the 1934 waterfront strike.

"Harry stood there," he'd point to an imaginary spot a few feet away, "and Hansy, a big German lad who never talked much, he was behind him...poor devil, killed by a sniper when we were in Spain.God rest his soul. Anyway, myself, I was in front with Harry, an' here come the cops, firin' that damned gas..."

On this Sunday, the old longshoreman was with his favorite niece in a gazebo on the school grounds and they were discussing all of their favorite subjects: political philosophy, literature, and baseball. The day was clear and warm and devoid of any activity more strenuous than the dragonflies hovering over the dahlias, and the daffodils blooming around the gazebo.

Uncle Con had lived with his wife Mary for many years in a small apartment on Valencia Street. Mary had died shortly before Pearl Harbor and his visits to Burlingame had become more frequent. He had no children, unless you counted Jack and Bob, his two Boston terriers.

Before boarding the street car for the long rumbling ride down the peninsula to Burlingame, he always stopped at the Star Bakery on Church Street to pick up some pastries. Pastries in hand, he rode in the back of the car where the door was kept open for people who smoked. The union doctor told him to quit smoking, and he did, but standing in the back of the car and breathing deeply was almost as satisfying as a couple of Chesterfields.

Sister Agatha finished the bear claw pastry before she spoke again. She touched the corner of her mouth with her handkerchief.

"Almonds, hmmm," she murmured before answering. "Well, to put it another way, Uncle Con, I think your Mister Marx has a very dreary outlook on the human condition. As I understand him, it's all about struggle and struggle and struggle. But is human history merely a story of struggle? For heaven's sake, is that the sum total of our human experience?"

"Ah, there you go, sneakin' heaven into the discussion already! Sneaky, Aggie, very sneaky."

They both laughed.

"Struggle is necessary, Aggie," he clarified as he poured more iced tea into their glasses. "Struggle is necessary because the rulin' class ain't about to give up what they stole from us by us just askin' 'em to do somethin' nice.

"Years ago, when I was just a lad," Buckley continued, looking into the hills beyond the school, "didn't I see that great man James Connolly himself speakin' in Dublin? Ah, that was before the Easter Risin' of 1916, when he was murdered by the Crown. Murdered! So shot to pieces they had to strap him up in a chair for the firin' squad…strapped in a chair, he was!"

The memory of the execution infuriated him.

"A pox on the blaguards who pulled the triggers," he spat out, "and them in London that gave the orders!"

Sister Agatha nodded and waited. Buckley shifted in this chair, and his anger subsided as he relived that moment in Dublin where the raw boned young laborer was one of a thousand workers in a public square listening to the labor revolutionary.

"Twas a glorious mornin', that day in Dublin, not a cloud in the sky over our heads. Even the wind had gone to sleep. I'll never forget what that great man said. I wrote it down that night. 'We must organize as a class,' he said, 'to meet our masters and destroy their mastership…'

"You know, Aggie, there were over a thousand people--a thousand, mind you--in the square, an' not a sound among them, you could hear the squeakin' of their shoes when they moved about. All quiet like—so we could all hear what he said. Ah, he was a grand speaker, our old Connolly, with his big moustache, wavin' his arms about like a windmill."

"Yes," Sister Agatha replied, "I agree, but we're still talking about 'struggle' and 'destroy.' Where is the place for the spirit and the God of love of the New Testament? Our Lord taught us to turn the other cheek and do good to those who hate us. These are not only our traditions, but many other religions also. What is the role of the human spirit? How does the spirit, or—if you will—the soul fit into your analysis? How does Mister Marx, or Mister Connolly, account for the power of human love?"

"Arra, you know me, Aggie, old Con Buckley. I believe in Groucho an' Harpo as much as I believe in Karl."

"Uncle Con, you are incorrigible!" she smiled. "Everytime I get you in a corner, you throw in a clinker like that!"

Sister Agatha sat back in her chair and exhaled melodramatically. "Now, tell me, how does your Mister Marx-- Karl, that is, not Groucho or his brothers —explain the striving of the human spirit toward a spiritual perfection?"

The two of them went at it for almost another forty five minutes under the gazebo, sitting or standing as the mood of the debate took them, frequently punctuated by gales of laughter when an important point was scored. The entire realm of human thought was in their field of fire, and they hacked at it with verbal scythes and shears. A small wooden table stood between them which held the plate of pastries, a pitcher of iced tea and two glasses to refresh dry vocal cords.

Carmen lay asleep under the table, stirring only when someone reached for one of the pastries. She knew she'd get one before the afternoon was over. Part of the deal with Maletesta was that Sister Agatha would look after Carmen. The two of them walking around the grounds had become a familiar sight on campus.

"Joyce," Sister Agatha was saying, "is without a doubt one of the greatest writers in the English language."

"Yes, but for an Irishman," Uncle Con interrupted, "he wrote a lot of babble, to my way of thinkin'. Myself, I prefer Sean O'Casey. Least I can understand him: 'the world's in a state of chassis!'" Uncle Con roared in laughter.

The nun laughed at their old shared joke, another epic mispronunciation of the King's English.

"When I was in high school," she said in a more serious tone, "my sister Maureen bought a copy of *Dubliners* which we read after mum and dad had gone to bed. It was more straight forward than his later work, but the genius was already there in that prose."

She smiled at the memory of those times at home.

A fly landed on Uncle Con's plate and he swatted at it with his cap, and Sister Agatha blinked out of her reverie at the sound.

"Your old dad would probably say it was like baseball," Uncle Con said, a smile forming.

"Joyce?" Sister Agatha asked, perplexed.

"All of it . . . life itself," the longshoreman answered.

"Well, yes, I think you're right," she considered, "for Dad, God rest his soul, everything under the sun was somehow related to baseball. Many's the time he said to me, 'now, you take baseball, Agatha, there's a sense of fairness in it.'"

"God, how he loved it! I remember that one Thanksgivin' when you were all out on Day Street, himself at the plate with his old bat…"

"Mum was so mad! The hot pies were cold when we got back for dessert. And he was talking about Highpockets Kelly and Tony Lazzeri…"

"An' your cousin Lefty, of course."

"Francis. Mum said that Lefty sounded like a gangster's name, so he will always be Francis in our house, if nowhere else in the world."

"Speakin' of baseball," Con began, "how about our former baseball player? An' the expedition?"

Sister Agatha closed her eyes tightly for a second. Then she opened them and grinned.

"Well," she began, "so far, so good, thanks be to God. The expedition left the town of Sibu two and a half weeks ago…"

One of the nuns came running down the path to the gazebo with an envelope in her hand. Carmen stood up and began the talking kind of singing which earned her name. Sister Agatha and Uncle Con also stood up when they heard her and looked up the path. The nun rushed up to Sister Agatha.

"I'm very sorry to interrupt, Sister—oh, hello, Mister Buckley--but it seems important.

The Western Union man just came," Sister Monica said breathlessly, as she handed her the envelope. She stood apprehensively. To her, telegrams were always bad news.

"Thank you Sister," Sister Agatha said. She sat down on one of the chairs and opened the telegram. Her eyes flickered back and forth across the paper. Her face turned ashen and she sagged in the chair.

"Oh no…no…oh, Blessed Mother, no…"

Uncle Con reached over and took the telegram from her fingers.

EXPEDITION ATTACKED BY HEADHUNTERS IN JUNGLE. STOP. I AM

BADLY WOUNDED. STOP. ALL OTHERS WERE KILLED. STOP. REPORT

WILL FOLLOW. STOP. SORRY. VAN VLIET.

SIXTEEN

Borneo

Maletesta plunged deeper and deeper into the jungle. Someone was following him. He stumbled blindly and fell often, tripping on the roots and slime of the jungle floor. The heat was oppressive and grew more stifling as the vegetation thickened around him. Thorns from creepers stabbed at his legs; vines smacked him in the face. He lost the Browning in his first fall in the muck, watching it sink in a brown colored pool as he heard his pursuers gaining ground. Luckily, he had not unstrapped his Ka Bar knife at the encampment, so it was now in his hand, slashing at vines and ready for defense.

He paused periodically to listen. The voices from the clearing were growing dim. They were gradually being overshadowed by the returning sounds of the jungle. He continued moving until, finally, there were no voices and the sound crunching and sloshing along behind him ceased. He collapsed against a dead tree to catch his breath.

He sheathed his knife and pulled out his handkerchief to dab gingerly at his forehead. Blood was still running into his eye. He wiped his face as best he could and held the handkerchief against his forehead to stop the flow of blood. He could feel the bump growing on his forehead where he had taken the blow of the war club. He watched his back trail.

God, my head hurts. What the hell happened? They were all over the camp in minutes. Hombardt. Willis. Goddamn ambush! A Goddamned ambush! Walked right into it. All those hired boatmen and porters.

He was growing dizzy as he picked through his thoughts.

Can't pass out here on the ground. Pigs, snakes, whatever.

The dead tree had many limbs. Laboriously he pulled himself up, grabbing branches with his right hand and pushing off with his legs. He faded in and out of consciousness. The tree creaked under his weight but seemed firm enough. Vines and creepers were gradually encircling the trunk and the limbs. For a moment they were snakes; then they suddenly became vegetation again. He shoved himself in between the trunk and three thick limbs and wedged his leg into the crotch of one of the limbs so he wouldn't fall out.

The dizziness returned. He noticed that his shirt was torn and the medal he wore on a chain around his neck was dangling on his shirt pocket. His mother had given him that medal when he finished boot camp. His dog tags no longer hung with it. He peered at it as if he had never seen it before. He held it in his hand. On one side was a worn-down image of Saint Christopher carrying the Christ child. He turned it over and read, *"I am a Catholic; in case of an accident please notify a priest."* He laughed loudly and maniacally.

"Is this an accident?" he shouted into the jungle, "or is it on purpose?"

He laughed hysterically and grabbed on to a nearby limb to steady himself.

An accident. Notify a priest. Just like that. So easy. So simple. Just like that. If only I was eleven again.

He heard birds in the limbs above him calling to each other. "What do you know?" he shouted at them.

So easy when you're eleven.

He began to cry, squeezing the medal tightly in his fist.

God, it was so easy to believe when you're eleven. So simple.

He felt the tree spinning around below him and braced himself for the nausea. Then he passed out.

Maletesta felt someone looking at him. He slowly opened his eyes. The dim light of morning filtered down through the jungle canopy, casting an unreal feeling on his surroundings.

He thought of one of those hollow Easter eggs that you peeked into from one end and beheld a shiny miniature landscape inside. The major difference was the rising heat and the cackle of the morning birds. And the never-ending buzz of the insects.

He located the eyes when he turned his head to survey his tree-bound domain. They belonged to a gibbon sitting on one of the limbs about twenty feet away from him. The gibbon was watching him, probably wondering what kind of creature this was in his tree.

"Good morning, Cheetah," Maletesta announced, "can you take me to the white doctor's hut?"

The gibbon scampered down the limb and leaped to another tree, disappearing into the foliage.

"Guess not. Oh well, it probably didn't work for Tarzan the first time either. Now, what the hell should I do?"

He lowered himself painfully to the ground. He had a rough memory of Van Vliet's map and where the last river was even though much of the immediate area was uncharted. He didn't want to return to the river because the attackers might still be looking for him or even may have left a guard behind for a few days in case he turned up. He took what bearings he could and headed in what he felt was the opposite direction of the encampment. Eventually he would be out of the jungle, hopefully near the highlands. A plan had not formulated itself yet, but instinctively he knew he must find the caves.

In his mind, they were no longer Hombardt's caves. They were now Sister Agatha's caves and he owed her that much. If he could find a river, he would take it to a village or some outpost of civilization to regroup. It was slow going and he was alone. Not like in the Philippines, two machetes working at one time, decent map, scouts, compasses, point men.

Well, at least there's no Japanese army to worry about. Headhunters? Those weren't headhunters who attacked the encampment. *They were hired killers, pirates, whatever. At least one of those guys was in the attack on the ship. So why the blowguns and native dress? Like a play. Doesn't make sense.*

The humidity was rising steadily, and the insects were on him again. He pulled the bottle of 6-12 out of his shirt pocket and then remembered that one of the porters had always helped him with the repellent. At first, it was quite a maneuver to uncap the bottle as he held it between his knees, turn it upside down shake some of the liquid on his hand by jiggling his knees, and wipe the repellent on his neck and face. However, as the day wore on, he became more agile with the procedure. He kept chopping with the knife as he slowly made his way through the jungle. His head was throbbing, but the blood of his wound had dried. He stopped regularly to drink from the vines full of fresh rain water. For a few minutes he thought that something was wrong with his head, that the day had passed and night had descended, but just as suddenly there was an opening in the jungle canopy and it was daylight again. An hour after starting, he came upon a creek, a shallow gurgle of running water.

"The rivers and creeks are the roads in the jungle," the scout Felipe Barreras had told him during their first sortie into the jungle. "They can take you some place, but they also take other people and animals some place too. You must always be alert."

His head still hurt but he was moving more carefully now, watching for danger, surveying before he moved. He listened. Felipe told him to listen to the monkeys. They would warn him if he listened close enough. He was not sure whether it was true or not. He was walking through a swarm of multi-colored flying insects when he thought again about the Malay pirates.

The pain in his head had lessened to a steady throb somewhere below the surface of his being. The expedition started to unravel itself in his mind.

The pirate attack on the ship...all right, that has to be part of it. That's for sure. And in Sibu, at the carnival...if Hombardt had only listened! Never mind, you can't go over that again. And now this...ambush. Now what? No one left but me...no one. Why? Then there's Van Vliet. Who is he? What's his game? Where is he now?

Maletesta didn't recall seeing him or Kwan in the clearing during the attack on the camp.

Why were the boats so old and the crew so inexperienced? It was almost as if they were expendable. Don't spend much money on men or materials if you're going to lose them. Simple economics. Only now, it adds up to murder. Why?

He remembered Van Vliet's antagonism toward him in the office and his attempt to cut him out of the trip. Later that night those would-be assassins chased him all over town.

Why?

He remembered the whodunits he had read while recuperating in the hospital. There was always a motive for murder, whether the detective was an English spinster or a tough-talking gumshoe. "Who profits?" the master detective would inevitably ask, and then came a list of suspects who were going to get something when Great Aunt Martha kicked the bucket. Not hard to figure out if you're writing the story.

Who profits from killing Hombardt? Or Willis? Or me? Can't imagine either of them had a large estate and nobody'll make anything off my death. None of it was large enough for somebody to hire crooked guides and pirates halfway around the world. Did someone want to stop the expedition?

Sure. He could see the headline: "Stanford University Contracts Pirates To Silence Rival Anthropologists in

Borneo." Sure. It didn't make sense no matter how many different ways he looked at it.

While he pondered the possibilities as he trudged along the creek, he grew careless.

He walked with his head down, thinking. He didn't notice that the jungle was gradually thinning out and becoming drier. The creek was growing wider and deeper, and was near the point of joining a small river when he saw the water buffalo.

The huge, slate-colored Carabao had been feeding when she heard Maletesta approaching. She stood six feet at the shoulder. Muscles rippled down her back as she raised her head. Her nostrils quivered at the smell of an outsider. From fifty feet away, the buffalo charged through the shallow water at Maletesta. He instinctively raised his knife and caught the buffalo in the left eye just before the animal's massive head rammed into his side, knocking him back against the river bank. The buffalo bellowed in pain and stood momentarily shaking her head as Maletesta struggled to right himself on the slippery rocks. He dropped the knife and grabbed wildly at the vines and roots covering the embankment, pulling himself up with all the strength he could command from his arm and legs.

Maletesta scrambled to the top of the slope aware of the snorting of certain death behind him. The buffalo was upon him again as he reached the crest and he rolled out of the way of the gouging horns. He rose desperately and leapt behind the nearest tree, the buffalo's horns almost catching his shirt. His head wound was bleeding again and blood was running down his nose.

He felt a sharp pain in his side with every breath he took as he dodged the buffalo around the stand of trees. The buffalo's head was also bleeding and froth gathered at her mouth.

She charged at the trees Maletesta ran behind in a dangerous game of hide and seek.

Around they went, from tree to tree, stand to stand.

Maletesta was tiring dangerously when he suddenly came to dry grass. The buffalo and he had played their cat and mouse game into more open country. There were fewer trees, so the buffalo changed tactics. Instead of charging, she waited, watching for him to make his move to the open.

The sun was bright overhead, a relief from the canopy of the jungle, but the heat rose and Maletesta's head began to swim. He stopped near one of the trees. He could not climb them because the limbs were either too high or his awkward one armed effort would make him instantly vulnerable to the buffalo.

Maletesta watched the buffalo waiting in the grass from the tree watching him. The animal had won. He could run no farther. He could not climb. Soon he would pass out from the wounds, the heat, and the lack of food.

Tears of frustration and anger splashed into the sweat and blood on his face.

"Where are you, Felipe!" he screamed at the sky, "why didn't your damned monkeys warn me!"

He glared at the stump of his left arm.

"God damn you, piece of shit! Worthless! Worthless! Why didn't I die with you and be done with it?"

He punched at the stump of his arm.

"Worthless cripple! Worthless!"

He punched himself hard in the leg. The buffalo, sensing weakness, moved closer. Maletesta felt something in his pants pocket when he punched himself.

What is it? The Zippo. My God, the lighter!

He looked at the grass in front of him, his eyes wide with a plan. Yes, the dry grass was thick enough and the wind was at his back. He took the lighter out and slowly crouched down, not wanting to warn his opponent. The buffalo was moving slowly forward. He snapped the lighter open quietly and thumbed the wheel. It sparked and lit. He held the flame to the thickest clump of grass, blowing on it at the same time. A puff of smoke, a crackle—within seconds the fire was going. He stood and looked over at the buffalo. Her nostrils were twitching; she was shifting her feet. The flames grew and spread and suddenly there was a four-foot long wall of fire moving toward the buffalo.

The animal turned and ran back toward the river.

Maletesta whooped and yelled.

"How about that, huh? How about that? Take that, *stronzo*! Fire, you know, like Alley Oop in the comics! Fire! Fire! Zippo! Ha, ha, ha!"

Maletesta danced away from the direction of the fire, watching the smoke and laughing wildly. He didn't see the gully and fell backward, dropping eight feet and landing in a dry wash. He screamed as he landed on his injured side with the pain burning through his body.

On the other side of the gully, a little girl stood looking at him.

"Hey, cowboy," she said, "don't worry, you'll be OK."

"Huh?" Maletesta said and lost consciousness.

SEVENTEEN

Borneo

He was floating in the air, looking down at himself.

No, it's not me.

He'd heard about this during the war. Guys he knew who were close to death. Then he was back. He saw the girl run away. He tried to get up, but he couldn't. He lay back and closed his eyes, trying to shut the pain out. He saw his left arm again. It was lying on the ground. Lonnie with unblinking eyes was applying a tourniquet below his shoulder. His whole side had gone numb and he was shaking. Bolts of pain ran up the arm and down his body. He looked at his bloody arm lying on the ground with his watch on his wrist. The second hand ticked methodically as it obliviously circumnavigated the dial. He felt himself vomiting.

The movement woke him. He was being carried in a rattan hammock by people he didn't recognize. He said something; he didn't know what, but the bearers were silent. He fell asleep in the swaying motion.

When Maletesta awoke it was night and he was in a longhouse. He was lying on a mat in a longhouse soaking in sweat. A dark skinned woman sat by him, watching him. Time passed and she was replaced by the girl. The girl grinned at him. He guessed that she was six or seven years old.

He tried to speak but his voice came out in a croak. He slept again. He had no sense of time.

During the day--or maybe the next day--he was fed some kind of broth by a woman. He opened his eyes as she held his head up to the bowl.

A white woman? No, couldn't be.

He thought he was dreaming again, but the broth seemed real. He coughed and some of it spilled. He felt the warm liquid drop on his chest, so he must be awake.

He saw a white woman with raggedly cut blond hair and dressed in old military fatigues. Her sky blue eyes watched him intently. She looked concerned and vaguely familiar.

I know: it's Ingrid Bergman. Sure. Ingrid, the Jungle Girl.

Maletesta startled when he heard her say, "rest now" and laid his head back on the mat. Then she left.

The next time he awoke, he could feel his strength returning. He checked himself over. His fever had broken. His ribs had been wrapped with rattan and there was less pain when he breathed. His cuts and scratches had been cleaned and were healing. He felt a poultice of some kind on his forehead wound and his head no longer ached. He was tired, but he was recovering and someone was taking very good care of him.

He began to take stock of his surroundings. He was in the sleeping quarters of a longhouse, but it was more simple than the Iban house the expedition had visited. The room was small and he guessed that the longhouse was also small and therefore he was staying in a village that was not very big. It was hot, but he did not feel the sticky humidity of the jungle, so he must be in the forests.

There was a mat hanging from the ceiling which divided the sleeping quarters from the living and eating quarters the same arrangement as was in the Iban longhouse. The living quarters seemed to always face an open verandah. There were times when he couldn't sleep and he just stared at the ceiling or listened to the rain. Sometimes he listened to the people on the other side of the dividing mat while they cooked and did whatever else they did.

They carried on long dialogues and sometimes monologues in their dialect. He guessed that the latter were telling stories because the speaker's words were often punctuated with gasps of disbelief or laughter. Once in a while he heard phrases of English from the little girl and--presumably--the white woman.

One morning shortly after he woke up, the girl came into the quarters and handed him a bowl of water. He drank all of it. The girl stood looking at him. Her eyes were bright and curious.

"Hi," Maletesta said, "what's your name?"

"Talah," she replied. She didn't move, but she smiled.

"Talah. That's a very pretty name. My name is John."

He set the bowl down and propped himself up on his elbow.

"Thank you for helping me. How did you find me?"

"I saw the fire. Same as the book."

"The book?"

"*Range War*, by J. Robert Manning. *A Story of the West*," she recited proudly.

"You're reading this book?"

"Finished it. Three times. Sentinel Books, New York, New York, 1924. Second Printing." She sat down attentively.

What is this? This is unbelievable!

"I see," Maletesta said, although he didn't.

Where did this girl learn English?

He heard the rain again on the roof. "What's the book about?"

"Dry-gulchin' rustlers!" the girl said fiercely. "They stole the cattle after the brush fire.

Then the cowboys got them back...you from Montana, John? Or Texas?"

"I'm from a city called San Francisco. But I worked on a ranch one time with cowboys."

"Shoot any rustlers?"

"No, we just chased the cows in Livermore from one pasture to another," he answered. "Sometimes I fell off my horse though," he confessed, laughing. Talah giggled.

"Why?" she asked.

"'Cause I wasn't a very good rider."

"Hmm," she said. Then she picked up the shoulder holster which was lying on the floor near the wall.

"This is for a six shooter," she announced triumphantly, "where is it?"

"Actually, it's for an automatic. An automatic pistol. I lost it in the fight. Lost my knife too. Made a real mess of things."

"Mess of things?"

Maletesta straightened himself up, grimaced with the exertion and then relaxed.

"You know, Talah," he said, "there's a couple of funny guys in the movies. You know . . . movies?"

She looked at him quizzically.

"Anyway, there's these funny guys. One of them is real fat and the other one's real skinny. They're always falling down the stairs, stepping into buckets of paint, driving crazy in their car…"

"Car?"

"Well…yeah. So, anyway, every time they get into some kind of trouble, the fat one says to the skinny one, 'well, here's another fine mess you've gotten me into.'"

Maletesta grinned at the punch line of his Laurel and Hardy joke.

"Me?" Talah said.

"No, the skinny one," Maletesta clarified.

"Oh," she said and laughed politely.

"Where did you get that book?" Maletesta asked, changing the subject.

"Tee Woo gave it to me."

"Who's Tee Woo?"

At that moment, the older woman came in, smiled at Maletesta, and said something to Talah in their language.

"She says you must sleep now," Talah interpreted, getting up. "Good-bye, John."

"Wait," Maletesta protested, "I have some questions."

It was too late. Talah and the woman were out of the sleeping quarter. He tried to pull himself up, but couldn't. He resigned himself to his lack of strength and lay back on the mat. Within minutes, he was asleep.

EIGHTEEN

Borneo

Maletesta sat on the open verandah, his legs dangling over the side. He was smoking a cigar one of the villagers had rolled for him from a local tobacco and palm leaves. After few pulls and some coughing, he decided it wasn't half bad. He had been up and about for two days now, living by gesture and Talah's translation, learning the ways of the people of this village who had rescued him. He had not seen the white woman since his first encounter.

For the past hour, he had been watching two of the villagers making a blowgun. Talah had told him that the first step was selecting the proper tree. The tree trunk was then split into several pieces which would eventually become blowguns. The pieces were laboriously rounded and smoothed with hand tools and sand until they became solid wooden shafts over six feet long.

Maletesta was watching the next part in the process: the drilling of the bore of the blowgun. A platform had been erected across the clearing from the verandah on which he sat. It stood about seven or eight feet off the ground and in the middle of the platform, a solid wooden shaft was held rigid, secured by rattan wrappings. One of the older villagers stood above the shaft, twisting a long iron rod down into its center. He twisted slowly and meticulously, cutting the bore into the shaft. A younger man poured water into the hole, keeping the wood cool and washing the chips out. They worked slowly and carefully, paying no attention to the hubbub of village noise and comings and goings around them. Periodically, they stopped and rested for about ten minutes. They were apparently the chief armorers of the village and took their duties very seriously.

Maletesta watched the pace of the work and decided that it must take several days to make a proper blowgun. Talah had explained to him, that, after the original cutting of the bore was finished, it was polished with sand until it was smooth and true enough to carry a dart to its intended destination. He knew from his reading that the darts held a variety of substances which could either kill or render unconscious. He had seen how effective they were during the ambush of the expedition.

These people began to fascinate him the longer he stayed with them. They accepted him unquestionably, sharing their food and quarters with him without a second thought. There appeared to be no orders given, yet everyone went about their chores without grumbling or apparent orders. They talked incessantly, whether they were repairing fishing nets, fixing the longhouses, weaving garments, or cooking.

Late in the afternoon of that second day, Maletesta noticed a stir among the villagers, a barely discernible movement. Throughout the village, people put down their work or stopped whatever they were doing and looked toward the trail opening to the forest at the edge of the clearing. Maletesta looked at the opening also. Within minutes, a hunting party emerged, coming single file out of the forest. The villagers erupted around them, yelling and gesticulating over the two large wild pigs which were strung on saplings and being carried by four of the hunters. In the middle of the party was the white woman.

Talah ran to greet her and then followed her to where Maletesta was sitting. She looked about forty years old and walked with confidence, her long strides covering ground in quick time. As he had noticed when he was recovering, her hair was cut short. Her skin was darkened from the sun, which made her blond hair all the more striking. She smiled. Her teeth were luminously white.

"How are you feeling?" she asked as she approached the verandah. Her voice had a low rusty quality, which reminded him of the sound of deep brooks in the Santa Cruz mountains.

"Fine," Maletesta answered, "thank you for your help."

He started to say something then hesitated.

"You know who I am, don't you?" she asked, matter-of-factly.

"I think so, but I can't believe it. Aren't you T.W. Wainwright?"

"Yes."

"You're supposed to be dead."

She had climbed up on the verandah as they were speaking and now she sat down near him, shaking her head and massaging her neck. She said something to Talah who disappeared, only to return a few moments later with some bowls of liquid. She offered one to Maletesta and they drank silently.

"Yes," Wainwright said finally, "dead to your world." She evaluated his improved physical condition and made a decision. "But, before any further explanations, I must know who you are and how you got here."

Maletesta hesitated and finished the liquid from his bowl. These people had saved his life; there was no way they could be involved in Van Vliet's scheme.

"I'm the last surviving member of an expedition which was ambushed back in the jungle," he answered slowly. "We were on our way to some limestone caves near the old Subu volcano when we were attacked."

"By who?" she asked.

"A gang of thugs. It's not quite clear to me how or why it all happened, but the thugs were dressed in tribal outfits and our guide was definitely a part of it. A man named Van Vliet."

"Why were you going to the caves?"

"We were an anthropological expedition. Funded by a college in California. We had evidence that something like the missing link might be found the caves."

"Missing link...hmm, yes, I used to like those stories." She sat quietly, remembering.

"What kind of evidence did you have?" she asked.

"One of the anthropologists had found some pictures of the caves taken by a Frenchman before the war..."

"War? What war?"

"World War Two, of course," said Maletesta testily. Then he realized that it had been seven or eight years since she disappeared.

"I'm sorry," he said, "I'd forgotten how long it's been since you disappeared, Mrs. Wainwright."

She waved her hand.

""Call me TW, or as my friends here say it, Tee Woo," she laughed.

She stretched and ran her fingers through her hair as if to bring up a memory she couldn't reach.

"'Mrs. Wainwight' died a long time ago," she said quietly.

"Now, who's at war? Is America in it? The Germans? I felt that Hitler would come to no good. And his pal in Italy, beating up the Ethiopians."

"Germany, Japan, and Italy against pretty much the rest of the world, although the Italians didn't account for much. It ended a year ago after four years of fighting..."

"Four years...my God!"

"There were battles in the Pacific, the Atlantic, Europe, North Africa, Asia...millions dead, cities and countries destroyed...surely, you must have heard something!"

Maletesta paused, frowning at her.

She took several deep breaths.

"From the river traders we heard there was some kind of war," she answered. "We knew the Japanese were in Borneo, but we had no idea of the scope of this war." She looked at her hands before she spoke again. "There's always a war going out there in your world. What happened in the end?"

"Eventually we won."

"Hitler?"

"Killed himself before the end. The other top Nazis are being tried for war crimes. I hope they hang all of them."

"What about Japan?"

"They were not going to surrender, so we dropped something called the atomic bomb on two of their cities. They surrendered quick after that."

"But they were allowed to keep their bases?" she asked.

"Heck no," said Maletesta, "they surrendered and the emperor quit. General McArthur is there now to start a new, democratic government."

"That doesn't make sense."

"What?"

"The Japanese have a base here, by the old Subu volcano. How can that be, if they've surrendered?"

Maletesta stood up. She must not have understood what he said.

"You mean the buildings are still there, deserted, stuff like that. Yeah, there are ghost towns like that all over the Pacific," he said.

"No," she replied, "I mean soldiers, drilling, patrolling, all the rest. A lot of them. Not far from the caves you talked about."

"It can't be! That's impossible!"

"It's there."

"No. It would have seen by a plane. Someone would know…" Maletesta blurted, beginning to pace on the verandah of the longhouse.

"It would be very difficult to see from the air. It's very well camouflaged," she noted, trying to alleviate his disbelief. "Hardly anyone flies over that area anyway. We are far, far away from everything, including the news. That's what I like about this place."

"How do you know it's there?" Maletesta asked accusingly.

"I've seen it. All of us have seen it at one time or another. We have to know where the soldiers are so we can avoid them. Thankfully, they don't seem to stray very far from the base."

Maletesta's pacing was more rapid. His right hand clenched and unclenched as he walked.

"You must take me there!"

"Why, do you intend to fight them singlehandedly?" She was looking very carefully at him.

"Yes! No, of course not, but I must go there…a Japanese base! It's impossible…and yet, and yet…kamikazes, divine wind…"

Maletesta's head was spinning, and he felt a chill come over him. He saw TW sitting on the floor watching him with concern in her eyes. The floor began revolving. He saw one of the villagers turn toward him, a look of alarm on his face. The images became blurred. He was falling…

NINETEEN

Burlingame, California

"And you've shown no remorse for your irresponsible actions!"

The Superior General continued to spit the words out. "You think you're better than everyone else, don't you? You don't have to account for your actions? You think nothing of making a laughing stock of the Order."

Sister Agatha sat stock-still, as the Superior General's verbal blows fell, her eyes blank, her thoughts to herself.

I saw Dingle Town
Frying Bantry Bay in a pan
And the whole earthly world
Turned 'round in an old water can.

The two nuns faced each other over a heavy table in the visitor's office at the school. Many conferences with concerned parents had been held over the old table. An aura of varnished authority hung over the table and the chairs on either side of it. Another nun, who accompanied the Superior General from the mother house in New York, sat back against the wall, taking notes on a spiral pad. Sister Agatha recognized her from somewhere in the past. There was no movement in the other nun's pinched face, but her eyes registered her agreement with the sentiments expressed by the Superior General.

Sister Agatha sat quietly, saying nothing. Her face sagged, and new lines seemed to have appeared overnight. She stared at a corner of the table, her thoughts yet again full of that fateful day when the news arrived.

"Uncle Con, I've killed them! I've killed them as sure as with my own hand . . ."

"No, Aggie, No! Don't go on like this. It's the kind of chance any expedition takes . . ."

133

The telegram was on the ground and the young nun who brought it burst into tears and ran back to the school.

"Any expedition?" Sister Agatha gasped, *squeezing the balled up handkerchief in her hand so hard that veins popped up on the back of her hand. "Any expedition? No, my expedition! I had to have it! My pride, my God-awful ambition, I had to have it!"*

For the first time in his life, Uncle Con was at a loss for words.

"Young Maletesta," she groaned, *"barely back from that horrible war...Doctor Hombardt...poor simple Mister Willis...oh, dear Jesus, will you ever forgive me?"*

Sister Agatha watched and heard her inquisitor, but she did not respond. The inquisitor cleared her throat regularly, and a fly buzzed near the window, periodically banging itself against the glass.

"...financial disaster. Do you think this Order is made of money? How will we ever recover?" The Superior General hammered on. "I just can't fathom it, Sister Agatha! How could you allow the Order and this college to have such public disgrace...such an embarrassment! What in the name of all that's holy were you thinking?"

The secretarial nun continued writing. Sister Agatha's stare shifted from the corner of the table to the floor. There was nothing to say.

Embarrassment. Is that all it is? All of them dead. Embarrassment? No new books. No laboratory. All of them dead. Embarrassment.

"We have received calls from prominent people who are very upset with the situation here at All Saints," the Superior General continued. "Several of our Trustees have even expressed a desire to leave...and they wish to leave with their resources! And what will we do about restoring the Building fund?" she sighed dramatically.

The Superior General shook her head from side to side in disbelief before she continued.

"You have provided a very poor example to the students, Sister Agatha, a very poor example. Especially with that disgraceful memorial service with an atheist, of all things! In all my time in this Order, I've never seen anything like this!"

Yes, the memorial service. Oh my goodness.

Sister Agatha had insisted on a memorial service. The math teacher, John Drillhart, had asked her if he could say a few words. Dear old Drillhart, laboring in the fields of higher math for over forty years. He was the first of the old guard teachers to come and congratulate her when she began instituting the academic changes. She suspected that his religious beliefs did not correspond with hers, but she never pressed the issue. He was simply the best math teacher she had ever known.

Drillhart wasn't a very articulate man. Sometimes his words poured forth ahead of his thoughts, but eventually they all caught up with each other and one realized he had said something particularly illuminating. Other times he hemmed and hawed as he sifted through a verbal quarry. He looked like an eccentric English don. His clothes were always on the verge of shabbiness and were assembled on his body apparently without a thought of color or material and smelling of pipe smoke, the cheapest roughcut brand he could find at the Owl Drug. The students loved him and knew he would spend whatever time they needed to clarify a problem or a procedure.

The memorial service was held in the campus chapel, shortly after the news had arrived from Borneo. Sister Agatha felt that the men deserved a proper goodbye, and that the students deserved an opportunity to express and experience it. She arranged for a Mass for the Dead by Father Enright, the campus chaplain, and told the faculty that simple eulogies could be given at the end of the Mass, if anyone felt moved to do so.

Old Professor Drillhart was the last to speak. The Chapel was full, even though summer session was in effect and a full schedule of classes was not being taught. The Mass had ended twenty minutes before, but the students and other faculty and staff remained in their pews. The silence was complete except for the occasional cough from the older staff and periodic sniffles from Maletesta's students.

Drillhart mounted the pulpit and wiped his eyes. They were always watery, so it was not clear whether or not the tears were for the deceased. He began with his usual opening stammer.

"I...I...I...thought about what I might say...on this occasion, harrumph and I, uh... looked in a book I have of eulogies. Ahem."

He scratched a spot behind his left ear.

"I read about people who died young...John Maletesta was young, but Dick Hombardt wasn't. It didn't seem appropriate. Then I came across some references to, ahem, religious martyrs and, well, that wasn't right either, was it?"

Drillhart paused again and tugged down the sweater vest inside his sport coat. Several of his faculty colleagues shifted uneasily in their pews or rolled their eyes surreptitiously at each other, but the students kept the faith, waiting for him to begin again. Sister Agatha sat in the rear of the chapel. She had been the first speaker and her words had been brief and choked. After she read the list of speakers to follow, she returned to the pew in the back.

"So," Drillhart finally started up again, "last night I put down the books and walked out onto my patio...as some of you know, I rent a small house in the hills over the reservoir.

"I looked at those stars out here...the planets...the solar system, and I thought about how we have tried to learn about them, ahem. I thought about Copernicus...Galileo...the ever-forward movement in our search for knowledge...to find man's place in this system...the human system...the scheme of things...uh."

Drillhart paused and pulled a blue polka-dotted handkerchief out of his hip pocket.

He blew his nose noisily and then shoved the handkerchief back in his pocket.

"Yes...as I was saying...uh...this pursuit of knowledge is vital to our very existence. Vital . . ."

He paused and looked directly at the students. His eyes were wide, and his gaze marched up and down the pews.

"Vital...the pursuit of knowledge is the reason for all education, the key, again, I say the key, to the progress of mankind...the ability to use our minds to reason things out, harrumph.

"This pursuit of knowledge for the ever-changing truth-- remember, it was once true that the earth is flat--is not without sacrifice: the sacrifice of Galileo to prove that the earth revolved around the sun, and in our own country, the sacrifice less than twenty years ago of a teacher in Tennessee who dared teach evolution. Yes, our search for knowledge involves sacrifice... unfortunately.

"And I list proudly in that group our colleagues who died in Borneo in the quest for knowledge of our origin...another sacrifice, a light to follow in the darkness. We grieve for them today, but, in our eternal quest for knowledge, tomorrow we must emulate them."

Abruptly, he turned and descended from the pulpit and hobbled back to his seat in the faculty section. The silence remained. No one moved. Minutes passed. Then Father Enright got up from where he was sitting at the side of the altar, walked to the altar railing and said in a loud voice:

"*Ete, missa est.*"

"*Deo Gratias,*" the congregation dutifully replied and began filing out of the chapel.

Sister Agatha's real problems began with the unfortunate circumstance that the religion beat writer for the San Francisco *News* had been on campus for a retreat that week and had dropped into the memorial service because he had a free period. His column "Christianity Today," which appeared in the Saturday edition on the following weekend, devoted the opening paragraph to the service.

"*Dead Teachers Compared To Galileo*" was the heading at the top of the column.

"*In a memorial service this week at the College of All Saints, the mathematics professor compared the teachers who were killed by head hunters in Borneo to Galileo and other 'heroes of science.' Other rubbish expounded by Professor John Drillhart was the evocation of Darwinist theories disputing the creation of man by God. One might expect this kind of agnostic nonsense from some secular college, but, really, dear readers, at the College of All Saints?*"

The telephones rang. The letters poured in. Parents threatened to pull their children out of the school. One benefactor withdrew his financial support with a letter saying he "had no idea such theories were being promulgated at the school," and that "until I am reassured that the College of All Saints is teaching true Christian values and not Godless atheism, not one cent will be forthcoming!"

Drillhart himself had gotten several letters accusing him of being a "communist sympathizer" and an "insidious troublemaker." He offered his resignation to Sister Agatha, but she refused to consider it. The flurry continued among the Catholic academic and business community.

Within a week of publication, Sister Agatha received a telephone call from the Order's motherhouse. A voice crackled through the line from New York. The Superior General requested her presence at a meeting, etc. She would arrive by train and be met by car at the Burlingame station, etc. No further communications will be held with anyone outside the Order, etc.

Sister Agatha shuddered and hung up the phone.

The call. And now this. Well, I can't say I don't deserve whatever punishment has been decided.

"...therefore, Sister Agatha," the Superior General summed up, "you are hereby suspended from your duties here at the College until further notice and will remain here incommunicado until another position for you can be arranged. During this time you will ask the Good Lord for forgiveness for your wicked deeds. Sister Martha will act as interim president. You may go now."

The Superior General sat still and cold with her final words. The secretarial nun finished her shorthand and looked up.

"*Deo Gratias,*" Sister Agatha murmured, as she was taught to reply to punishment. Then she stood up and walked slowly out of the office.

"Pride goeth before the fall," the Superior General stated when the door closed. The other nun said nothing. She wanted to say "uppity bogtrotter" but kept it to herself.

As Sister Agatha left the Administration building, Carmen fell in step beside her, buoyantly at first and then, sensing her mood, she dragged her tail and lowered her fine black head.

"It's all right, Carmen," Sister Agatha consoled. "It's all right. Good dog."

She reached down and stroked the dog on her back and Carmen sprung to life again.

Then the two of them walked across the Common to the convent.

TWENTY

Borneo

The drumming and the chanting stopped abruptly on a signal from the headman. Two young men faced each other across the fire in the center of the clearing. They each held a long-bladed parang and a shield made of rattan and animal hide. On a second signal from the headman, they shrieked and charged around the fire at each other, swinging their parangs.

The shorter man delivered the first blow with the flat side of his parang. It was parried by the other with his shield. As he parried, he leapt forward and swung his own parang at the shorter man's head. The blade was met by a shield and the shorter man darted back, grinning widely. The rest of the villagers sat in a rough circle around the two warriors. They cheered and gesticulated as the demonstration continued and the two men dodged and struck. The drums had begun again, adding to the excitement.

"Too close for comfort," Maletesta shouted to TW Wainwright. They sat cross-legged on the ground next to the headman and his family.

"Oh, there might be a few nicks, but no real harm done," TW explained, smiling. "You get used to it."

There was a roar from the crowd and they both looked back at the young men. The shorter one had tripped and fallen backwards on the ground. He rolled quickly as the other warrior swung his parang downward and sliced into an exposed tree root where the first man had landed seconds before. Unfortunately, his blade clung fast to the root so the shorter one jumped up and whacked him on the buttocks with the flat side of his blade. He yelped and the crowd laughed uproariously. Then both men fell to laughing uncontrollably, with the "injured" man making a great point of rubbing his buttocks in mock pain.

As the hubbub died down, Hulang, the headman, stood up and called an end to the confrontation. It was the last of six dances, each of which varied in ferocity and movement.

The village, which Maletesta had estimated numbered about eighty men, women and children, broke up into smaller groups as the festivities continued. The drummers were joined by flutes and singers and dancers.

Maletesta and TW moved away from the heat of the central fire and sat on a log near Hulang's longhouse. It had been almost three weeks since the village had retrieved Maletesta from the jungle. In several conversations, he tried to tactfully bring up the subject of her disappearance. Each time, she had steered away from the topic.

"Why?" he suddenly asked.

"Why what?"

"C'mon! You crashed, what, eight, nine years ago? You could have come out of the jungle any time. The war didn't stop you. You didn't even know it was on. And yet you've stayed here obviously, with these characters who aren't too far removed from cave men. Why?"

TW looked at him calmly and didn't say anything for a few minutes. Maletesta shifted on the log nervously.

"I suppose brashness goes with youth," she said. "I'm no longer used to frontal attacks with words. I suppose that's another one of the reasons why I'm still here."

"I apologize. I just can't figure it out, that's all. You were on top of the world! We all followed your flights in the newspapers. I used to cut the headlines out and paste them in a scrapbook: *TW Wainwright, First Woman to Fly Solo Across the Atlantic Ocean.*"

She smiled slowly but said nothing.

"You were in the movies," he continued, relentlessly. "You were on magazine covers. You had a rich husband. My cousin went down to Union Square to get your autograph when you appeared in San Francisco. Waited two hours in line. I couldn't get out of school or I would have been there too."

"Yes," she said, a slight smile appearing on her face, "I remember that time in San Francisco. San Francisco was genteel. It was harder in other cities. The shoving and pushing, you know, 'if I can but touch his cloak I will be saved'..."

"So," Maletesta interrupted, "what happened? According to the whole world, you crashed in the Pacific. They searched for weeks. Our Navy, the British Navy...everybody who had a boat or a plane. Not a sign, no wreckage, nothing."

"They were all looking in the wrong area, apparently. My navigational equipment failed during the storm, and I got completely turned around. Then we lost radio contact, so I flew dead reckoning. I guessed we were over Borneo and I thought there would be an airstrip on the coast near Brunei."

She stopped and looked at the ground in front of them. She picked up a small twig and looked over at Maletesta. Then began peeling the bark off it with her fingernails absentmindedly. She could hear the motor of her plane spluttering.

"The fuel gauge was on empty and I told Rusty Magowan, my navigator, to grab his parachute and jump. He refused. 'Oh no, he said, we've come this far together and we'll finish this ride together.' Rusty had his maps on his lap and was trying to find a reference on the ground. We knew we couldn't make the coast.

"The engine stopped. Then it started up again. I could see a clearing below on the edge of a forest, so I went for it. 'Hang on, Rusty, I yelled' and he began laughing. I couldn't help it, I started laughing too. At about 500 feet, the engine quit for good. A tail wind picked us up and I overshot the clearing. We hit the edge of it and skidded into the trees."

She was silent again.

"When I woke up, I saw three natives looking in the cockpit at me. I ached all over.

The plane was a mess…"

"Magowan?" Maletesta asked softly.

"Dead. A branch from the tree that finally stopped us came through the window and killed him."

At that point Talah came up to them and gave them each a bowl of rice wine.

"Tee Woo and John," she said excitedly, "you must come. You are missing all the fun! Too much talking!"

"Thank you, Talah," TW said, "we'll be back there soon."

"Okay," she replied and scampered back toward the gathering.

"She speaks English well," Maletesta noted.

"She adopted me shortly after she came to live in the village. Her parents drowned in a monsoon. She is looked after by these people--they are like one big family--but we kind of hung together like two orphans. She also helps me in my work."

"Which brings us back to my original question: why? And, secondly, what kind of work is this? I mean, you could have done movies, owned a flying school, written a book--the world was at your feet."

Maletesta pointed over to where the villagers were continuing their festivities.

"This is work?" he asked, with an incredulous look on his face.

"John," she replied, "John, there is still so much for you to know about the world."

He didn't say anything. After a moment, she spoke again.

"You mentioned my appearance in San Francisco. It was one of many: Chicago, Dayton, Pittsburgh. My book was selling well; the publisher arranged the tour..."

She stopped speaking. He could see a glistening in her eyes.

"It's ok," he said quickly, "if you want to talk some other time..."

"No," she said, clearing her throat. "John, in Chicago, they were pulling at me. Do you understand? Pulling at me!"

"Pulling at you?"

"They would have torn me to pieces if there wasn't a line of policemen around me," she stated flatly.

"Oh."

She stood up and began pacing slowly, her hands in the side pockets of her fatigue trousers. They were obviously part of goods traded on the river with Chinese merchants who ventured into the interior periodically.

"Where does one start?" she asked rhetorically. "Did you know that they were going to name a candy bar after me?"

"No."

"Yes. The Wainwright bar. '*Flies High in Taste*' was the slogan. Nougat, almonds, peanuts, salt, sugar, and chocolate. With coupon to send in with three wrappers and fifty cents to receive your souvenir photograph. Do you know what?"

"What?"

"I hate candy."

Maletesta laughed. She was still standing, sipping the fiery rice wine from the bowl. She hadn't yet learned to like it but accepted it. In the light of the full moon, he saw her crooked nose and strong chin in silhouette, the boyish chop of her cowlick driven hair. He thought about the scrapbook and the pictures of that face he had laboriously pasted in it on the kitchen table at home. The only other scrapbook he had was of DiMaggio.

"And your husband?"

Maletesta's question broke the silence between them.

"Bob?" she answered. "Poor Bob. He wanted to marry a hero. Poor Bob. Through some misfortune of fate, he picked me."

"Yes, well..." Maletesta stammered.

"Do you know something about him?"

"He...uh...got married again. A movie actress..."

"Good. Somehow I knew that would happen."

She turned toward him.

"I wasn't a hero, John. I just wanted to fly where no one else had flown before. That's all."

"So, why stop flying? Why haven't you tried to get out of here? Why?"

"I'd climbed all my mountains. There weren't any left. There was nothing except public appearances, candy bars, and a husband who didn't love me and whom I didn't love. I was becoming a freak in the side show. Come see the world famous flier, one dollar. See her laugh. See her cry."

She stopped abruptly.

"It's time to go back to the celebration," she said and began walking in long quick strides back toward the fire.

"What exactly are they celebrating?" Maletesta asked as he caught up with her.

"A different kind of hunting party is going out tomorrow. Dangerous."

"Why?"

"John Maletesta! Is 'why?' your middle name?"

"Yes, and I want to go. These people saved me, but I'd like to know the reason for this hunting party. If it's dangerous, I want to help them."

"I can see why that nun wanted you on that expedition. You don't give up easily. I'll ask Hulang if you can go. He understands your retribution type of thinking. One of our people was killed yesterday while he was fishing. I believe Hulang will try to kill only one in the attack. These people have a belief in balance."

She stopped suddenly and faced him.

"Maybe it's as simple as that. There's a kind of balance here. And for me, peace."

Then she turned and she and Maletesta walked over to the group where Hulang was sitting. It was quieter now. Most of the youngsters were asleep as were some of the following day's war party. The fire was growing dimmer and a tribal elder, Honlee, was telling a story. They sat at the edge of the group around him.

"Will it be rude if you translate it for me?" Maletesta whispered to TW.

"Not if I do it quietly. Listen up."

Hulang was smoking a hand rolled cigar as he spoke. He was a handsome man with straight black hair and eyes which Maletesta thought were always filled with curiosity. Like the rest of his people, he was only a few inches over five feet tall. Honlee sat next to him.

"...and when the boy was at the river," Honlee continued and TW translated, "he saw a crocodile and asked, 'grandfather will you take me across?'"

"No, I cannot," the crocodile answered.

"But, why not?" the boy asked. "If you don't carry me, I'll have to walk all the way up the river to cross the log."

"Then you should start walking," the crocodile said, "because if I carry you, I'll have to eat you."

"Oh," the boy said and began walking up river.

The last line was greeted with gales of laughter by small gathering. As the laughter continued, TW explained to Maletesta that the crocodiles were highly revered by the villagers and even thought to be dead ancestors, but stories like this were told so that people did not take the beasts for granted.

When the laughter subsided, the elder sitting next to Hulang began to tell his story. He was older and thinner than Hulang and Honlee. Maletesta had not seen him before. TW whispered that his name was Keelun, and he was the village wise man. Keelun spoke in a clear but reedy voice.

"One day," he began, "a beautiful bird flew into the longhouse of a man who had no woman. The man asked the bird, 'What do you want?' The bird said to him, 'You must not go with the others to make the pulp of the trees into food. If you do, you will never find a woman.'"

Then the bird flew away.

"The next day he did not go to the river with the others to beat the inside of the tree trunks into food. When they came back, he was sad and stayed away from them. He went to see the wise man, but the wise man said nothing.

"The next day and the next day, the man stayed in the longhouse while the others went to the river. When they came back, they were angry. They went to the headman and said, 'he should not eat, he is not helping.'

"The headman said, 'he is not eating; he is very sad.' Then the headman said to his daughter, 'I do not know what is wrong with him and I must help with the fishing nets today. Go and see him and tell me what is wrong.'

"So the headman's daughter went to see the man. But when she went into his longhouse, the man did not see her, but the beautiful bird. 'Why have you come?' he asked and the headman's daughter answered, 'To help you.' Then he saw that it was the headman's daughter. And she stayed there with him that day and on the next day, they both went to the river to make the trees into food."

There was no laughter at the end of the story, just general murmur of agreement. It was by now very late in the night and most of the villagers had drifted away. The fire was nearly out. Hulang and Keelun stood up, which was the signal that the celebration was over.

Keelun leaned on a staff made of wrapped bamboo. Maletesta watched him as he limped away from the group. Keelun's right leg was deformed and withered and it took a great effort from his left leg and the staff to move him from place to place.

"Since birth," TW said quietly, noticing Maletesta's attention to Keelun. Then she took him by the arm and turned him around to face her.

"John Maletesta," she said, looking him squarely in the eyes, "you might give this some thought. That man was chosen at birth to be the wise man, the holder of all the village's knowledge and beliefs, because he was deformed. Because he was deformed, he was special. Earlier you said something about cavemen and civilization?"

She headed toward the longhouse and then turned back.

"Oh, Hulang said you may go with the war party tomorrow. Good night."

TWENTY ONE

Borneo

Dow stood resolutely behind a tree a few feet off the footpath and watched the bend in the trail which led to the enemy village. He held his parang tightly in his right hand and his shield in his left. It was his first challenge as a young man, but he showed no uneasiness. His only movement was in the blinking of his eyes.

Back in the undergrowth, the rest of the raiding party waited in silence. Maletesta crouched down next to Hulang. He held the parang they had given him and watched the trail. Every once in a while Hulang looked at him and smiled. The other four hunters were equally still, even though the ever-present flies were continually landing on them. Maletesta thought of another time in the Philippines and another ambush. He trembled quietly and then willed his body to be still.

The plan was explained to him earlier that morning before the party left the village. It was a simple matter of revenge. A young man from Hulang's village had been killed by a hunting party from another village while he had been fishing alone. Now Hulang's party was going to kill a man from that village.

"Why just one?" Maletesta had asked through his interpreter, Talah. TW was not present at the pre-attack meeting in Hulang's longhouse.

"Only one is necessary. Only one was killed," Hulang replied.

"No," Maletesta stated, "you must punish them. Then they won't attack one of your people again!"

"Punish?" Hulang asked.

"Kill their warriors. Burn their village. That's the way you fight a war."

Maletesta then explained some of the battles of World War II to them and how his company had operated behind enemy lines in the Philippines. At times he gestured violently with his hand, and Talah imitated his gestures as she translated. At one point in the description of a particular ambush, he swept away a mound of sand which he had formed in front of him. Talah gleefully did the same. Hulang and his party sat attentively as he spoke. Occasionally they nodded or murmured to each other.

When Maletesta finished, Hulang and his hunters were quiet for a moment. Then they could contain themselves no longer. They burst into laughter. They held their stomachs and rolled from side to side and laughed loudly and gleefully.

Maletesta was perplexed. He was describing battles in the greatest, bloodiest war in history and they were laughing. Talah tried to take both sides, alternately looking stern like Maletesta and then grinning with the warriors. When the laughing finally subsided, Maletesta asked what was so funny.

Hulang smiled at him as if he were a simpleton.

"Only one is necessary," Hulang repeated, and they began gathering up their weapons for the journey.

Maletesta was thinking about the conversation as he squatted next to Hulang in the underbrush watching the trail.

These people are nuts.

However, he approved of the plan as Hulang had explained it to him. Dow, the youngest of the party, would wait until someone from the village came down the trail and then step out of the forest and challenge him. It was Dow's job to kill that person. Then Hulang's party would return to their own village after Dow took the dead man's head. If other villagers or more than one hunter came down the trail, they would stay in hiding. Waiting for the one hunter was good training for the young Dow, Hulang had explained to Maletesta. The rest of the party were there in case something went wrong and others came to attack Dow.

Maybe there is a kind of sense to it after all.

Maletesta watched two women from the other village walking on the trail. There was a creek about a quarter of a mile from where the ambushers waited and he guessed the women were going to bathe. The women went by the unseen hunters and another half hour went by.

Suddenly, another young man appeared at the bend in the trail. Maletesta tensed and felt an imperceptible movement from Hulang beside him. He could not see Dow.

The young man was about Dow's age and carrying a spear in one hand and a woven bag in the other. Possibly he was going fishing in the creek. His gait was brisk and his face was unworried. He had not learned to watch as he walked.

Dow stepped out onto the path and faced the other man. Maletesta could now see both of them. They were about fifteen feet apart. The man had stopped abruptly when he saw Dow. He was not sure what to expect but quickly brought his spear up to a defensive position. Dow growled something that Maletesta did not understand but he understood the hostility in the tone of the voice and the stance Dow was now taking on the path.

Dow spoke again and shook his shield at the other man. Then he drew his parang back menacingly and spit. The other man did not hesitate.

Without a word he dropped the woven bag and, with both hands on his spear, took a step toward Dow. Dow began circling him to the right, drawing invisible circles in the air with his parang. The other man followed Dow's movement, rotating counterclockwise, his spear at ready. He did not call for help. Their eyes were locked to each other as they slowly executed the circular dance. Birds called overhead. Insects buzzed around them. The morning breeze rustled branches overhead. The two men heard nothing except the quick movement of their breath rattling in their nostrils and the scrape of their bare feet on the dirt path.

Suddenly, Dow made a rush forward, waving the parang and shouting. The other man lunged with his spear, but Dow quick-stepped back and dropped to one knee. He parried the thrust of the spear with his shield, and, as he parried, he leapt forward swinging his parang. Dow's blow caught the man from the other village just below the rib cage, slicing deep into his side. The young man clutched his side with his left hand and let the point of his spear drop to the ground. Dow swung the parang again. This time he hit the jugular in the neck and blood spurted forth. The man collapsed to the ground, dying. He still had not uttered a sound since Dow had first sprung from behind the tree.

Dow stood over him, breathing heavily. He was not aware that Hulang was now standing beside him until Hulang said something to him again. He saw his older warriors around him, smiling. His adversary was lying below him, his blood moistening the dirt of the path under their feet. Then he realized what Hulang was saying, and he leaned down to take the head of the dead man. Maletesta stood next to Hulang. A shiver ran over him as he watched Dow deliver three blows to remove the head from the dead man's body.

With Dow carrying the head by its hair, Hulang's party melted back into the forest and began the return journey to their own village. Maletesta trudged behind, deep in his own thoughts.

TWENTY TWO

Borneo

"One more, John, one more, please!"

Talah shouted the translation of the children's yelling over the cacophony of noise coming from the seven children who surrounded him. They were sitting on the ground between two of the village's longhouses. It was the first clear day after more than a week of rain.

During the monsoon, Maletesta had used his parang and a coarse stone to carve a top out of a piece of hardwood. It had been slow going, holding the hardwood between his knees when he used the stone or wedging it into a tree trunk when he used the parang. The finished product was not an object of beauty, but it spun pretty well. Now he was showing the village children how to spin it with a thin length of jungle creeper. Talah held the top upright while Maletesta pulled the creeper which was wound around it. Gales of laughter and screams erupted as the top went spinning off on a flat rock in the ground.

"You show them, Talah," Maletesta said as he rose to a standing position, "my thumb's about worn off." He gave the thumbs up sign to Talah and she returned it smiling.

"She likes you, John," TW said. She had come up behind him as he was getting up.

"She's a real pip," Maletesta nodded, "and she's got lot of spunk. Smart as a whip, too."

"C'mon, John, let's walk. We've got some talking to do."

TW led off in her long legged canter, and Maletesta fell in beside her. He was now completely recovered from his injuries, and his willingness to assist the raiding party three weeks earlier had endeared him to the village. He did chores like the others and had even learned to tie knots in the fishing nets, though the procedure with one hand was laborious. He absently wondered if his new found ability could be applied to shoes. Sooner or later his slip-on boots would wear out if he stayed here. He would test his shoe tying again when he got back to the States. Maletesta was convinced that at some time he would be back home in San Francisco, but he hadn't given a thought to the details. He was obsessed with the existence of an actual Japanese base not far away. He wouldn't believe it until he saw it with his own eyes.

TW stopped at one of the longhouses and was greeted by several of its occupants who were on the veranda weaving rattan.

"I'll only be a few minutes," she said to Maletesta as she began climbing the log ladder. "I set a boy's broken arm here the other day and I want to take a look it."

When TW emerged from the longhouse, they continued their walk, eventually finding themselves on the high bank of the river which lay several hundred yards south of the village. She sat down on a large outcropping of rock on the bank.

"All right," Maletesta blurted out as he turned toward her, "I'm waiting. I need to see that base. When do I get taken there? I'm fully recovered, thanks to you and these people."

"John, you have a one-track mind."

The water gurgled below them. It was so clear that they could see fish making their way along the river bottom.

"I used to think it was a sign of character, but I'm not so sure anymore," she continued.

"Call it whatever you like. I've got to see that base!"

"Why?"

"Because I think it has something to do with the ambush of my expedition. The expedition I was supposed to protect. I'm convinced Van Vliet was behind the ambush and, since there's apparently nothing else in this jungle, there has to be some connection to the base."

"No other reason?"

"What?"

"No death wish?"

"Death wish? Why? What do you mean?" Maletesta shot back, the corner of his lip turned up like a trapped hyena.

"Come off it, John! I've seen it in you. I've seen it in men like you . . . 'the gravely wounded hussar charged the cannon.'"

Maletesta took his time to light a handmade cigar. The Zippo was just about out of fluid and he had to thumb the wheel several times before it flamed.

"You're not sure, are you?" she continued.

She watched him blowing smoke over the river, saying nothing.

"Good," she said shortly, "because I have a proposition for you."

"A proposition?" he asked warily. "What kind of a proposition?"

"It's about Talah."

Maletesta crushed out the remains of his cigar under his boot.

"What about her?"

"I want you to take her out of here. Back to the States with you."

"What? Are you kidding?"

"No, I'm perfectly serious. Now, stop waving your arm around for a minute and sit down and listen. Please, John."

The tone of her voice had changed completely from any of their previous conversations. He sensed the urgency in it and sat down on some gnarled roots opposite her. He watched her suspiciously.

"As you know, Talah is an orphan. Her parents were from another village and were drowned during a monsoon. One of our hunting parties pulled her out of a swollen river. When they brought her here, Hulang readily welcomed her, as he did me and you. However, she has no family here so there would be no objection to her leaving."

TW paused.

Maletesta stood up and walked over to the bank. He picked up a stone and tossed it into the river. He picked up another and threw it farther.

"But why?" he asked. "I thought you felt that life here in the village was just about the nearest thing to heaven you could find. Or are you coming back now too?"

"No. This is where I want to spend the rest of my life. I know that, and you know that."

She twisted a vine in her hands.

"With Talah, it's different," she said after a moment, "I've...I've grown quite fond of her, John. Maybe she's like the daughter I never had. She's very bright, as you know. She knows the healing ways. She sees things, she's..."

TW stopped again, but this time he waited for her to continue. She dropped the vine and pushed her hands through her hair. Her words tumbled out in a rush.

"John, she's about seven years old. If she stays here, she'll probably be a mother in nine of ten years. Civilization and all the diseases that come with it are closing in on these people. The chances are she won't live past her fortieth birthday, if she's lucky."

"But that goes for all of them," Maletesta stated.

"Yes, I know, but there's no way we could take the whole village out."

TW stood up and looked back toward the village.

"Nor would they want to go," she continued. "And I'm not sure that they should. What we have here is something that is very beautiful. But it is dying…"

Maletesta saw a tremble go through her body. She coughed and then turned to face him.

"Perhaps," she said, "it will live through Talah. *If she has the chance.* If you will take her out of here and raise her as if she were your own daughter."

"My own daughter? Are you nuts? I'm not even married!"

"I think you're a pretty big man. There's good stuff in you, John Maletesta. That nun, what was her name?"

"Sister Agatha."

"She was no fool."

"Well, she gave a cripple a chance, and he flubbed it."

TW walked over and stood in front of him, her blue eyes blazing.

"Flubbed it? You were ambushed! You can't blame yourself for that! What is the matter with you?"

"You don't know what you're saying!" he shouted back at her. "I don't know anymore! I don't know what I can do anymore. This is crazy!"

"Oh…fie on it!"

With that, TW strode off back toward the village. Maletesta threw a few more rocks and watched them glance off trees across the river. Then he kicked at the ground and grunted. Then he walked back to the longhouse.

Throughout the afternoon, he found that he was watching Talah surreptitiously.

If I took her back to San Francisco, what would I do with her? Should she stay with mama and pop? Where would she go to school? God, the whole concept was incredible! Would I be like a father? No, I'm not ready for that. She'll stay here. Really, how would I ever take care of her? On my teaching salary? Hell, I probably won't even get my job back. Do I want my job back? That's another question. Well, she is a nice little girl anyway.

Toward evening, he saw TW again. She smiled that smile of hers at him, and he knew that she was no longer angry with him. A hunting party brought in three small deer that afternoon so there was much feasting in each longhouse that night. When the festivities were over, TW asked Maletesta to join her in her compartment of the longhouse.

"You have to come to grips with that," TW said after they had settled down on the mats. She pointed at the pinned up sleeve of his left arm.

Maletesta bristled.

"I have," he said, "Is that all you wanted?"

He got up to leave.

She grabbed his right arm and held it tightly.

"No! You haven't! And don't leave!"

Begrudgingly, Maletesta returned to his position on the mat and scowled. She looked at him and rolled her eyes. He tried to suppress a smile unsuccessfully.

"That's better," she said. "Let's not start where we left off. Now what did you do before the war? Were you working, or were you in school?"

"I was in school," he replied gloomily.

"What kind of career were you studying for?"

"I was a political science major, but I was actually studying baseball," he answered, his eyes lightening. It was the first time he had expressed his educational experience so clearly.

"Oh." she said and understood. She looked directly into his eyes and said, "You were good, weren't you?"

"I was damn good."

"What position did you play?"

"Centerfield. Hit .406 my sophomore year."

"Were you planning to try out for the major leagues?"

"I already had," Maletesta brightened, his memory back in those glory days before the war. "The Seals, that's San Francisco's minor league team, called me for a tryout. Joe DiMaggio played for them and Frankie Crosetti and Lefty O'Doul! And they called *me* to come down for a try out at their Stadium. At 16th and Bryant. Where my pop took me to see DiMaggio during his 61 game hitting streak…

"They put one of their best pitchers up against me, Al Lien…"

The words came pouring out, his eyes glistening.

"Al Lien! Ha! I clobbered him! Two home runs, four sure doubles, five easy singles! All their top brass were there to see me. This reporter from the *Call* was there, and he kept yelling at me from behind home plate, 'you're the next DiMaggio, kid! You're the next!'

"When I came away from the plate, I couldn't talk. I thought I'd burst. I…"

He stopped suddenly. He'd sworn to himself never to talk about it again. He squeezed his lips together and looked down at the mat. He watched a small blue insect running along the edge.

A silence fell between them again. Minutes passed. A light rain was ticking on the roof over head and there were some soft murmurs of sleep on the other side of the partition. Light flickered from the stub of a candle, one of the trade items acquired from the Chinese river merchant who also pulled teeth.

"I could have been somebody," he said finally.

"How old are you?"

"Twenty-four."

"Just a baby."

She waved a hand at him when he started. He relaxed.

"You know," she said in her low melodical voice, "Keelun the shaman is probably about fifty. No one counts years in the tribe. I find that refreshing. Back in the States, they'd undoubtedly say I was too old to be a candy bar now."

They both laughed at the absurdity.

"I might have been a half Baby Ruth," Maletesta said. He was rolling a cigar one-handed with the local product and a large leaf.

"Keelun," she said, "was trained by one of the elders when he was a boy. He was trained in the ways of the spirits. They believe that all things, living and not living, have a spirit in them. The academics who study religions would classify them as animists, but, for me, that's too simple a definition"

"My grandmother was a little like that. I never knew whether she was serious or not," Maletesta said, "but she'd talk about winds that were nasty and winds that were good. One time she fell in her garden, and she said the rocks caused it. Everyone else said it was because she was old."

Maletesta lit the cigar with the candle stub and a pungent aroma filled the room.

"Keelun was selected to be shaman because of his deformed leg..." she said.

"You told me that already. What's the point? Unlike the ancient Greeks who put weak children out on a flat rock to die, these people find a job for the cripple. So?"

"Not a cripple. They regard his deformity as being marked by the spirits for special accomplishments. For one, Keelun knows more about healing than the chief physician of the medical center back in San Diego," she said.

"I saw him collecting plants the other day," Maletesta said, exhaling smoke toward the roof.

"Not only healing by herbs, although that aspect of it fascinates me too. What I'm trying to learn is the healing of the spirit."

"Yeah. Father, Son, and Holy Ghost: whoever's first get the most."

"Don't scoff, John. It misses the point."

TW stood up and stretched, breathing deeply.

"So," Maletesta asked, "do you want me to go to Keelun for some kind of healing?"

She sat down again, closer to him on the mat.

"No. You're not quite ready. All I want you to do now is to realize that this man, with his deformed leg, is one of the most important members of this tribe. I want you to see that."

She caught his eyes and held them. He looked down at the cigar in his hand.

"All right," he said reluctantly.

The rain had been steadily increasing its tempo on the roof as they talked and the sounds of the storm swallowed the smaller sounds of the adjoining rooms of the longhouse. It was as if the two of them were alone in a universe of rain.

"Do you have a sweetheart, John?" she asked.

"No. Not anymore."

"What was her name?"

"Annemarie. Why?"

"Annemarie. A pretty name. Is she pretty?"

"Yes."

"When did you last see her?"

"She came to the VA hospital. I told her to leave."

"Any letters?"

"I threw them out. Then I guess she finally wised up and stopped writing."

His cigar had gone out, so he set it in one of the bowls near the partition.

"You're too young to be so hard, John," she said quietly.

"If I'm hard on myself, it's my business, anyway."

"Yes, but you're also hard on other people. You've shut them down." She paused and then said, "and you're shutting yourself down..."

"Goddamnit!I don't have to listen to this..."

Suddenly she leaned over and kissed him lightly on the lips. He reached out and pulled her close, feeling the warmth of her body next to his. He pressed his lips against hers, and they fell back onto the mat. He ran his fingers through her hair and then down her neck. She sighed and threw her head back like a spring mare. He fumbled with the buttons of her shirt, but she squirmed away from him and pinched out the candle. Then she rolled back to him and pulled him down upon her.

TWENTY THREE

Borneo

They awoke at dawn and Maletesta began talking softly, lying on his back and watching a spider weaving in the bamboo roof beams overhead.

"They told me the dreams would stop eventually, but they haven't. I see my arm on the ground, the second hand of my watch ticking like nothing changed. I feel the blood pumping out. Lonnie's BAR blasting…I hear myself screaming."

Maletesta 's voice droned on like a litany, without color, without accent.

"You must give it time," she said.

He turned his head and smiled at her. Then he began again.

"The landing was horrible…I'd never seen anyone die before. But the first ambush was worse…I'm supposed to keep everyone safe; I'm the officer.

"I can't forget Billy Rankin. 'I'm from Great Falls, Montana,' he'd say. Put his hand out. Big smile. He had a chipped front tooth which reminded me of a beaver in a cartoon. He was barely eighteen. Only shaved once a week. Took a lot of kidding about that. 'Hey, Billy, is this your day to shave?'

"His dad was on a road crew for the WPA. Billy wanted to be a mechanic. Talked about engines all the time. Camshafts, carburetors, pistons; it'd drive you crazy. He had just gotten a job at a garage in Great Falls when he was drafted." Maletesta stopped.

TW waited.

Maletesta inhaled deeply, exhaled and began again.

"We were lost, separated from our company. It was not too long after we landed. We were tired, and we got careless. We were going through a grove of trees and ran right into the

Japanese. We all opened up except Billy. He was on my left. He just stood there…I don't know why…I've thought about it…I don't know why…he just stood there."

Sweat appeared on his forehead. His eyes were transfixed to the roof beams. The spider continued her weaving. TW squeezed his arm gently.

"We just fired, like instinct. We weren't even aiming. Bullets were whining all around us. There was no other sound except the firing, no yelling, nothing. Then it stopped.

"The Japanese had run for it. There were a couple of them on the ground…I looked for Billy. He had fallen where we were when we first saw the Japanese…he…he…"

He closed his eyes and swallowed hard twice.

"Billy was lying there, holding his chest. His rifle was on the ground next to him. He hadn't fired a shot. Blood was seeping through his hands. They were kind of clutching, but barely moving. I knew he was hurt bad. His face was white and his eyes were looking around. There was nothing I could do…there was nothing I could do!

"I tried to help him sit up. He was saying something but I couldn't hear. I took off my helmet and leaned closer. He said, 'this ain't right, lieutenant, this…'"

Maletesta was silent, breathing deeply.

"He screamed, 'Mommie! Mommie!'

Maletesta swallowed hard.

"And then he died. I was holding him."

TW gently wiped his brow with a cloth.

"It was my platoon. He depended on me. And I let him down."

Tears rolled out of Maletesta's eyes and down the sides of his face.

"Sleep now, John, sleep," she said, and he tried to resist it but he fell into a deep sleep. She watched him sleep for almost an hour. Her mind was a jumble of thoughts.

Maletesta. War. So young. Caught between death and life. He's got to let one go to begin the other. Like I did. Can he do it? Can I trust him with Talah? Somehow I know I can. And he's all I have. Without him, she'll never be able to leave. Look at my hands. They had always been square and short. Now they're rough and calloused from work in the village. I like these hands. I like it here. I'll die here. When? It's not important. Not anymore. Only life is important.

Life and Talah.

TW remembered that today was a fishing day and left the room.

The rain had stopped and the sun was high in its track when Maletesta emerged from the longhouse. He had slept all morning. He was hungry, but he felt strangely peaceful. He played for a while with the children and then went down to the river after one of the old women told him through gesticulations that many of the villagers had gone fishing.

The fishing methods used by the villagers fascinated Maletesta. Netting was familiar to him, and it reminded him of the part-time job he once had with the Vattuone Brothers who supplied a lot of the crab to the Fisherman's Wharf restaurants. He had also seen pictures in the *National Geographic* magazine of primitive people fishing with spears. During his stay in the village, he had seen them using both methods. Today, however, a new method was being employed. The villagers were throwing little balls of rice into the river several hundred yards upstream. After the fish ate this bait, they appeared to die and float to the surface where they were picked up by villagers standing in the shallows downstream and placed in baskets slung over their shoulders. He spotted TW working with the collectors downstream and sloshed out to talk to her.

"Are they dead?" he asked when he was alongside her. He smiled awkwardly. He was unsure of how he should be acting.

"No. They're only stunned. The rice ball contains a plant which causes them to lose consciousness. Pretty clever, eh?"

"Yeah. I should bring some back to my friends who fish in the Bay."

He helped her collect a few more fish which were floating toward them. The women around them were singing a slow song while they waited for the fish to come to them.

"Their songs remind me of the rain," he said.

"Yes," she said, stooping to grab a fish.

He could feel the pebbles in the river bed with his toes and the cold water swirling around his calves. He watched the villagers working in unison, singing softly.

"What if I want to stay?" he asked quickly.

"Stay? You mean, here?"

"Yes, uh, to be with you…"

She sloshed over to him and hugged him gently. The women near them giggled.

"John," she answered, looking squarely at him, "your place is not with me and not here."

The river flowed around them.

"I…uh," he began.

"No," she said, putting her finger on his lips, "this is my life. You must get on with yours."

She moved away from him and returned to picking up fish. He left the river and carried one of the already-filled baskets back to the longhouses. When he came back, she was still in the river.

"Well," he said, "I'm ready."

"Good," she replied, "ready for what?"

"I'm ready to go to the base."

She placed a fish in the basket. Two furrows appeared between her eyebrows and her lips tightened. She sighed. "All right. I know nothing I can say will stop you."

"No."

He picked up another fish and put it in her basket.

"I will talk to Hulang about it this afternoon. I know he will give you a guide or two to
show you the way."

"OK. Thanks."

He caught her gently by the arm as she sloshed by him.

"You know, I have to do this," he said.

She looked at him for a moment and watched his eyes look away. Then she reached down to pick up a fish. When the last of baskets were almost full, one of the women signaled upstream and the baiting stopped. Soon the remaining fish floated to them and were collected and they all started back to the village.

"What about Talah?" TW asked as they walked along the path.

He stopped and shifted his feet, looking at the ground.

"I don't know quite how to say this, but, well, you know, I…" he began.

"I'm counting on you, John Maletesta."

"I don't know anything about kids!"

"Nonsense! I've watched you with the children here. You become like one of them. They love you! Besides, I'm sure your Sister Agatha would help. And your parents."

"They're old."

"How old?"

"I don't know. Forty-seven, forty-eight."

"Phooey! Try again."

She was smiling. He kicked at a rock.

"I don't have any money. A teacher's salary barely covers my room and board," he said triumphantly.

"Talah is an heiress."

"Huh?" he scoffed. "I thought you said she was an orphan! What heiress?"

"She is. Come back to the longhouse with me. I've got something to show you."

Back in her room at the longhouse, TW picked through some baskets in the corner. She pulled out a small oil skin pouch and turned to Maletesta.

"Hold out your hand," she commanded.

When he did, she opened the drawstring of the pouch and carefully shook out four rubies. The gems lay glistening in his palm, caught in a beam of afternoon sun which had found its way through a gap in the rattan wall.

"Holy cow," he whispered, his eyes aglow.

"If you know anything about rubies, these are pigeon blood, the finest. And, therefore, the most expensive."

"Where did you find them?"

He shifted his palm and the light in the rubies changed.

"Talah had these with her when she was pulled out of the river," she recounted, remembering the event. "She had a bag around her neck which must have belonged to her parents. This pouch was in it with some hairpins, shells, pearl buttons, and other odds and ends."

"Did anyone see them?"

"Of course. There are no secrets here, and she wanted to show everyone what her parents had given her."

"What did they think?"

"About the rubies? They took turns holding them up to the sun and watching the lights. They laughed, and then they got tired of the exercise and went back about their business."

169

She smiled at his shock over the village's reaction to the rubies.

"After all," she explained, "they're only bits of colored glass. You can't eat them. You can't hunt or fish with them. They won't keep you dry…"

"All right, all right. Expensive colored glass, though."

"I think it's enough to take care of her until she's grown up, through college."

She gathered up the gems and put them back in the pouch.

"And then?" he asked.

"And then she's on her own, just like the rest of us."

They were sitting where they had lain the night before. She sighed and a look of forlornness passed quickly through her face. She took his hand in both of hers.

"John, you can't let me down on this," she said. "When you leave here, there will be no way I'll ever find out what happened. I want to know in my heart that it's gone right."

She released his hand.

"It will," he said finally, "but the rubies must stay here. The time may come when they will be needed."

TW knew not to protest. Maletesta stood up.

"Now, will you talk to Hulang?"

TWENTY FOUR

Borneo

"Very good...very good!" Maletesta exclaimed, nodding his head and rubbing his belly. He licked his fingers and reached into the coals to pick up another piece of meat. Yoon and Pwan, the two villagers Hulang had assigned to guide him, sat crosslegged on the other side of the fire chewing and smiling at him. They had killed a small deer that afternoon and what was left of it was sizzling in the coals of the fire.

Maletesta wished he could speak their language.

Yoon and Pwan were easy company, and the three of them enjoyed the impromptu sign language necessary for communication. They had been walking for three days and were getting close to the Japanese base.

Earlier that day, Maletesta called for a halt in a clearing and knelt down in the dirt. Yoon and Pwan watched attentively as he proceeded to make a relief map on the ground. He pushed dirt into mounds and piled up rocks to designate mountains. With a stick he scratched deep furrows into the ground which became the rivers they had followed or crossed. Then he piled up some broken sticks to indicate their village and the Japanese base. He left the base separate from the rest of the map and drew a rising sun flag in the ground next to the sticks. He knew that they recognized the Japanese flag because they pointed at it and made angry faces. Yoon and Pwan were delighted as he explained with directional pointing and charades of crocodiles and monkeys how the map worked. They clapped as he acted out the three of them slapping at insects while going through a swamp the day before. Periodically, Maletesta paused in his presentation and asked them in hand signs to point out the theatrically-recreated spot on the relief map. It was a technique he learned in the Philippines. Many of the people he met in the back country could not understand a map on paper, but quickly grasped a relief map where they could see the physical representations of the world around them Yoon and Pwan were fast learners. With their help on the map, he estimated that they would be close to the Japanese base by tomorrow afternoon. They also placed the base at the foot of the old volcano, Mount Subu, just as TW had told him.

After they finished the last of the deer, Yoon and Pwan curled up around the fire and slept. Maletesta lay on his back. He could see patches of starry sky through gaps in the canopy of branches overhead. The jungle was less dense here and drier, more like the highland village they had left. He thought about his mission.

I was hired to protect Hombardt and Willis and I didn't. They're dead, just like the rest of them. All those boatmen who weren't boatmen. Hired cheap to be targets for a setup. Why? I smelled a rat in Sibu, but I couldn't make it stick. Now I'm back fighting World War II again? Or am I? Do we go back to the beginning to begin again? Is this the completion of some circle I can't see?

He placed another thin stick on the low fire and watched it simmer and crackle. He stared at the small spurts of flame erupting along the stick.

Does anyone know I'm not dead? Poor Ma, she must feel awful. And Pop. There's no way I can get word to them until I get out of here. Sister Agatha. Where is she in this circle? My circle. What the hell is it? Nothing makes sense!

The stick was a bright ember now. The brightness mesmerized him. The light within the light, burning in the dark.

TW. Talah. It's all so damned confusing. Can we all leave together? No, she won't go.

I've got to settle this base thing first. I must see that base! I must know what the hell's going on!

Why the ambush? Something to do with the fossils? Where's Peking Man? Bastards! Are they hiding out there, waiting to start the war again? It can't be! It has to be a mirage or something. The dead people aren't a mirage, you chump, you've got to find out. The base has something to do with the ambush. It has to. Well, you'll know soon, Gianni, won't you? The die is cast? Yes, the die is cast.

Finally Maletesta fell into a restless sleep. Images of Japanese soldiers chasing him across a baseball diamond. Closer and closer, catching up with him. He reached the bat rack and pulled out a 42 ounce bat. He turned to face them, trying to swing the bat with his right hand. He couldn't bring it around, so he tried to grab it with both hands. He looked down and there was no left hand. The soldiers were on top of him. He screamed and jumped up.

Yoon and Pwan were both up on their knees, looking at him wild-eyed. He knocked on the side of his head with his knuckle and smiled weakly. He gestured them both back to sleep and lay down again. He stared into the dark, listening to the night sounds. Something was rustling in the bush near them. There was scampering in the branches. Eventually, he went back to sleep and didn't wake until morning.

At full dawn the three of them took to the trail again after a light breakfast of the cold rice they carried with them and some mangoes.

Mount Subu grew larger and larger as the trio made their way closer through the bush toward it. The hilly terrain was flattening out and the thick cover of the morning began to thin as they closed on the mountain. The trees were less dense with more waist-high brush interspersed throughout the grassy meadowlands. They moved more slowly and carefully as the day opened up, aware of their increasing lack of cover.

When they stopped for a small late-morning meal of fruit, they were very near the area where Maletesta would leave his guides as arranged and continue on his own. This had been explained to them by Hulang with TW translating. He did not want to jeopardize these people for the sake of his own curiosity. The three of them sat in a grove of ironwood trees as he showed them on the ground where he would go and where he would meet them at nightfall. He only needed a few hours to scout the base and return.

Maletesta, Yoon, and Pwan moved out of the grove after they finished their planning.

In front of them lay several hundred yards of meadow with low brush and then another wooded area. Once in the open, Pwan stopped and turned to the other two, wrinkling his nose. Maletesta sniffed. He smelled only the aroma of flowering shrubs they were stepping through. Pwan smiled and pointed toward Mount Subu and pinched his nose with his fingers. Maletesta sniffed again. This time he caught the faint odor of something like sulfur. Pwan made a rumbling noise in his throat and laughed. Yoon gave him a serious look and he was quiet. Yoon then took the lead. He walked slower than usual.

They picked their way carefully down the trail through the meadow, mindful of the fact that the Japanese base was only about a mile away. Yoon was one of Hulang's best hunters. His sight and his hearing were very acute and during this trip he had seen or heard danger long before the other two. On one occasion he had seen a crocodile lying in the undergrowth upstream just as Maletesta and Pwan were about to wade into the river. Today he was growing more apprehensive, but he had not seen anything to justify his concern.

While the trio was maneuvering through the brush of the meadow, Talah had reached the spot in the ironwood grove where they had stopped for their meal and planning. She could see them moving through the trees and knew that she would wait until they were well into the woods before she left her cover. She had been following them since a few hours after they left the village.

Talah watched Maletesta closely as the one-armed man pushed through the brush. She had found him when he was dying and would always protect him. It was the way her parents had taught her. When Talah was younger, she had taken a small bird from a nest before a snake could get to it. "Now you must take care of it," her father said, and he made her a bamboo cage for the bird. She fed the bird and eventually it grew strong and tried to get out of the cage.

"Now you must let it go," her father said and she did. As she watched Maletesta, she thought about her father and the bird. She did not know if it was time yet. During his stay at the village, she was never very far from him but he hadn't noticed.

The trio was going through the meadow single file. Yoon stayed in the lead, pausing frequently to look and to listen. He carried his spear loosely in his left hand, casting left and right as he led them. Maletesta was about ten feet behind him. It was approaching noon and growing hotter and he was sweating lightly. Pwan took up the rear, several steps behind Maletesta, carrying a blowgun. All three had parangs strapped to their waists.

Not too far from the wooded area was an outcropping of rocks ten or twelve feet high. Yoon stopped here to wait for Maletesta. He turned and smiled as Maletesta plodded on. Maletesta looked up and saw Yoon hurled back, as if he was hit by a giant invisible fist. Instinctively he dropped to the ground when he heard the rifle shot. A second bullet slammed into Yoon and he rolled off the rocks dead.

Goddamnit! Snipers! Goddamnit!

As he dropped to the ground, Maletesta glanced back to Pwan and saw that he was confused. Pwan could not see anyone and was too slow getting down. He shook his head when a bullet buzzed nearby, reacting to it as if it was a flying insect.

"Get down!" Maletesta yelled at Pwan, but it was too late. A bullet hit him in the side of the face and he crumpled to the ground.

Bastards! Where the hell are they?

From the delay in hearing the reports from the rifles, he guessed they must be at least two hundred yards away.

Screwed up again, Maletesta! Goddamnit! Both of them dead! How many people die because of me! Wake up, you shit head! Goddamnit! Wake up! Get to those woods ahead. Can't go back to the grove. Too far.

He squirmed on his belly through the brush to the other side of the rocks. He lifted his head up enough to see the lay of the land between the rocks and the woods.

Not much cover, damnit.

He started forward gingerly. A bullet ricocheted off the rocks over his head. Another one kicked up a mushroom of dust about twenty feet in front of him. He scrambled back behind the rocks.

Now where to?

Maletesta looked back toward the ironwood grove. Then he saw movement in the brush between the grove and him.

No.

He was being cut off.

Only one choice. When you can't go north, south, or west, you go east toward the mountain. Higher brush, maybe I can dodge them.

Maletesta raised himself in a low crouch and took off through the brush to the east. He ran a ragged pattern.

Red Grange, the Galloping Ghost! Down, back, left, right, right. They're firing the wrong way now. Left, hook, left.

The soldiers were plunging through the brush behind him and firing, but they were firing blind, into the brush around him. Suddenly, the firing stopped. He didn't wonder why.

They've lost me, ha!

He kept running. He knew he was close to thicker cover where they would never find him.

"That's quite enough, Maletesta. You can stop now."

That voice!

Maletesta pulled up abruptly, his chest heaving. Standing in front of him were Van Vliet and Kwan, smiling. Both had their rifles aimed at him. He caught his breath, breathing deeply.

"Son of a bitch!" he spat out between desperate gulps of air. Van Vliet laughed.

Back at the edge of the ironwood grove, Talah watched in horror as Yoon and Pwan were shot down. Then she saw the Japanese soldiers and another white man capture Maletesta. She watched them lead him off toward the base. She followed carefully.

TWENTY FIVE

Borneo

"Talah is gone! I can't find her anywhere!"

TW almost shouted to Hulang, who was sitting outside his longhouse mending a net. He looked at her calmly, thinking that he had not seen her this upset in all the time she had been in the village.

"How long?" he asked.

"I don't know for sure. At least a day. I thought she was in another longhouse when she didn't sleep in ours last night. Today I needed her to help with young Tan's broken arm. I looked all over and I couldn't find her!"

"She's gone after the man she saved," Hulang said. "I understand it."

"Yes, but she's only a child!"

"She knows the forest."

"What about the soldiers? How close to the soldier's place are Yoon and Pwan going?"

"They are not taking the young man all the way to the soldiers' place. When they are close, he will go by himself. And then come back to them."

"I am worried for her, Hulang," she said. "I am worried for her."

"I will call the others."

Hulang called the three other elders and the Keelun, the wise man. He was not bound by their advice, but heeded it as a necessary consensus in their small village. When they met it was late afternoon. The women brought food, rice wine, and smoking leaves to them. They talked and they ate and drank and smoked until it grew dark. No one was allowed to interrupt or disturb them during the meeting. TW grew tired of pacing and couldn't eat, so she went down to the river. She sat near the spot where she and Maletesta had last talked.

When she came back, there was a flurry of activity in the village. The young men bristled with excitement. Images flew by her, projected by cooking fires and candles. Women and children scurried about in the longhouses making preparations. An agreement had been reached in the meeting. The elders and the Keelun had assumed the worst. A party was being sent out at first light and, since there might be extreme danger, Hulang himself was going to lead it.

TW cornered Hulang near his longhouse.

"Hulang," she said, "I must go with the party."

"No," he answered, "you cannot. Some may die. All may die. Who will know the medicine?"

"Keelun."

"Keelun is old. You will stay."

There was no appeal from his decision. She returned to her longhouse and sat out on the verandah for a long time. Other women came and sat by her, saying nothing. In the morning she met with members of the party before they left. She had trained young Dow in her first aid knowledge, but she was no longer sure that it was superior to the remedies that the village had used since time immemorial. Nevertheless, she handed Dow what was left in the kit which had survived the airplane crash years before. It contained a dwindling collection of needles, thread, and bandages. She hoped the kit would come back unused.

The party, ten strong plus Hulang, left the village quietly. The hunters of the morning were more somber than the play actors of the night before. There were no more ferocious mock encounters between the youngest members. Hulang's gravity set the tempo for the party.

TW watched with the other villagers as the young men disappeared silently into the jungle track. Then they went about their daily work.

TWENTY SIX

Borneo

Maletesta could barely see his hand in front of his face. He had been thrown in a cell in what he assumed was the fort's stockade. It was damp and without light, but there were holes in the wall near the ceiling where he could feel fresh air.

So they don't intend to suffocate me. Thank God for small favors.

He had scanned the fortress as they led him into it from the woods. It was very ingeniously designed and built. He entered through the main gate, which was only wide enough for a tank, several of which he saw inside the compound. The front wall and about half of the side walls appeared to be concrete, but it was difficult to tell because they were covered in jungle creeper. The walls were also built into trees which provided overhead cover and served as lookout towers. From what he could see as they marched him to the stockade, the entire rear wall and the side that were not concrete were the mountain itself. There were many trees inside the compound which had not been cut down. Their canopies, when connected with the camouflage netting on the building roofs, made the fort invisible from the air.

The fortress reminded Maletesta of a bandit hideout he had seen in one of the Saturday matinee serials at the Royal when he was about eleven years old. The weekly serial was about jungle bandits and they had a hideout which was hidden in a mountain. The bandits would hold up a bank in town, then flee into the jungle. When they came to the right spot, they'd pull a branch down from a tree and a secret door would open in the mountain. Their pursuers would always ride charging by the secret door. It wasn't until the last chapter that the hero found the secret door, after the bandits had kidnapped his girlfriend.

Maletesta and his friends built a hidden fort in the tree in his backyard and played for hours on end, ambushing neighbors on their way to the grocery store, blasting enemy Chevrolets as the rolled down the street, retreating to the invisible safety of their stronghold. It was a fond memory. Stick rifles, cap guns, hand-painted flags...

"Are you awake in there?"

The shutter in the door had been pushed back, letting a bright shaft of sunshine into the room. Maletesta jumped in surprise.

"Well, are you there or not?"

It was the voice of Van Vliet. He was apparently standing outside the door out of Maletesta's view from the straw cot on the floor.

"Who wants to know?" Maletesta answered truculently. There was laughter outside the door.

"I've come to say goodbye. You should have better manners...or at least curiosity," Van Vliet laughed.

Maletesta stood up and walked over to the door. The cover of a grate in the middle of the door had been opened. There were two bars in the grate about five inches apart. He squinted through the opening into the glare. He guessed it was about ten o'clock in the morning the day after his capture. He had not been given anything to eat. He saw Van Vliet and Kwan on the other side of the door. A Japanese guard stood several feet behind him with his 6.5 Arisaka rifle held at ready.

Van Vliet was smiling. The guard's face was impassive. Like the soldiers who had captured Maletesta, the guard's uniform was showing signs of wear, but his rifle was well-oiled and his eyes shone with duty.

"The war's over," Maletesta said to the soldier.

"Don't waste your time. None of the soldiers understand English," Van Vliet said.

"Tell me, old boy, how did you get through the jungle alive? Did you swing from tree to tree like your friends, the orangutans?"

"None of your business, you treacherous son of a bitch," Maletesta said quietly, his voice barely above a whisper.

"What, no voice?" Van Vliet snickered, moving closer to the door. "First no arm, now no voice?"

Van Vliet broke into gales of laughter.

"Why?" Maletesta rasped.

"Why? Why?" Van Vliet repeated. "Because it was there! Isn't that what they say?"

Van Vliet was enjoying himself immensely. Then he suddenly became serious.

"Money, of course, my young fool. What else gets men going? Women? You can buy them. Power? You can buy it," he paused. "Colonel Tamako pays me to keep fools like you and the others out of this piece of Borneo. He has other plans for it. Maybe he'll tell you about them before he kills you…oh, you'll get along famously. He's soft on orangutans too."

"More people will come looking for those caves," Maletesta whispered again.

"Caves?" Van Vliet snorted. "There ain't no caves, bucko! Honestly, Maletesta, it's a shame I have to leave today and miss your execution tomorrow morning. You've provided a bit of entertainment for all of us, you know."

Van Vliet began laughing again.

"What's so funny? What do you mean, 'there ain't no caves?'" Maletesta asked.

"Colonel Tamako blew them up when he was building this place. Stitched 'em up forever under the volcano. It was just bad luck that those old photographs turned up in that idiot Hombardt's hands. All the other dope on those caves has been destroyed. Even in Sibu, you won't find any information about them. Nowhere. Nothing. Not even in Government House."

"You're a liar."

"Yes, that's true. But what I've said is also true," Van Vliet answered, grinning proudly. "We are very thorough. You're a teacher, aren't you? A teacher should appreciate that. We nicked all the cave files at Government House. Every one of them. Get this, we even let the clerk on duty live because a dead man would arouse more suspicion. We had to rough him up a bit," Van Vliet paused. "Ah well, he didn't have much of a mind to begin with anyway."

Van Vliet snickered at the recollection.

"Le Boo," Maletesta confirmed quietly.

"What?" Van Vliet exclaimed, surprised and inadvertently moving closer to the door.

Maletesta's hand shot through the opening in the door and grabbed Van Vliet by the neck.

"This is for all of them," Maletesta whispered. His fingers tightened around Van Vliet's throat. Van Vliet's mouth was open but no sound came out. His eyes were bulging and the color began to change in his face. He grabbed weakly at Maletesta's arm, trying to break the grip. Maletesta had inherited his father's big hands, and his grip was complete. He watched with cold eyes as Van Vliet's knees buckled and he began to sink slowly to the ground. He pulled Van Vliet closer to the door in able to keep the death grip on the collapsing man.

Kwan and the Japanese guard were also taken by surprised by the quickness of the movement and it took them several seconds to comprehend what was happening. When they came to their senses, they smashed at Maletesta's arm with the butts of their rifles. After the second blow on his wrist, Maletesta released his grip and drew his arm back into the cell.

Van Vliet dropped to the ground and the guard slammed the cover on the opening shut. Kwan knelt down and began efforts to revive Van Vliet. They could hear Maletesta laughing inside the cell.

"It isn't over yet, you Dutch bastard!" Maletesta called from the other side of the door.

Van Vliet was gasping and gurgling. Kwan held him from behind in a bear hug and was lifting his chest and releasing it as Van Vliet gasped and gurgled. In a few minutes he was breathing more steadily and able to talk.

"Tomorrow you'll die, you crippled pig!" Van Vliet screamed hoarsely. "You'll die! Die! No carnival to hide in! You'll die! And when I come back three months from now, I'll piss on your bones!"

"Bacci mi culo," Maletesta spat back.

Van Vliet staggered away from the cell leaning on Kwan's shoulder as his strength and normal breathing returned. They stopped under one of the trees in the compound where their backpacks and Van Vliet's rifle were stashed. They hoisted on their packs and, with the rifles in hand, Van Vliet and Kwan exited through the main gate of the fortress. It was a walk of several hours before they would arrive at the place on the river bank where they'd left their boat. The Japanese soldiers who were crossing the compound while going about their duties paid them no attention. The guards at the gate did not salute.

Maletesta was getting hungry. He decided that he would try to sleep to get his mind off his hunger and rejuvenate his strength. He could see dimly in the gloom, having some faint light provided by the crack under the door. He kicked some straw together and lay down. There were insects rustling around him but he was too tired to care. His wrist hurt.

A fracture maybe? Nah.

He rubbed it on his thigh.

It was worth it. Almost got him. Would have been sweet.

He couldn't sleep because he kept thinking about food. Not any food, but a corndog, of all things.

A hot dog on a stick! Soaked in mustard. Playland at the Beach. The roller coaster. The bumper cars. The diving bell. A hot dog on a stick. Deep fry corn meal batter with a hot dog inside. On a stick.

Maletesta could taste that first bite through the batter into the dog. Ah. His mother would raise an eyebrow but buy him one anyway.

I must think of something other than corndogs. Who's the commander of this place? Tamiko? No, I think it was Tamako. Is he insane? Must be, not to want to surrender when everyone else did.

He dozed off thinking about corndogs and reading about the surrender in the hospital newspaper.

He was awakened by the sound of hammering outside in the compound. Somebody's building something.

Well, why not? How else do you keep soldiers busy when there was no war to fight?

He heard commands being shouted; materials dropped on the ground. He stretched himself up to the air holes and listened. He couldn't see because the holes were purposely cut at an angle. He could hear hammering and sawing now. Suddenly, the cover on the grate in the door opened and a command barked out in Japanese. Though he didn't understand it, he recognized the unmistakable cadence of a military command.

To hell with you. Come and get me!

The command was repeated.

Curiosity overcame him and he moved slowly to the doorway. He looked through the opening. A young officer was standing outside, flanked by two soldiers. When he saw

Maletesta appear at the opening, the officer smiled, grasped his throat with one hand and pointed with his other in the direction of the hammering and sawing in the middle of the square.

Maletesta turned his head in that direction.

My God! They're building a gallows!

The officer smiled again, saying something in Japanese.

"The war's over, you nutcake!"Maletesta yelled. "Over! *Finito!* The Emperor surrendered. General McArthur runs your damn country now!"

The officer closed the cover on the grate in the door.

"Listen to me, you *cretinos!*" he yelled at them through the door. Then he kicked it.

"Easy, Gianni, easy," he hissed to himself and began pacing around the cell.

If you're going to find an opening at all during the next twenty-four hours, you'll need to keep your temper. Calm down. Calm down. All right. Do the old drill. The enemy and you. Count up their resources: manpower? One hundred men. Maybe. Enough room for that many. Equipment? Well armed and well trained. Discipline? Without a doubt. Well led? Probably. Tamako must be a powerful officer to keep these men here and convince them the war is still going on. Well led? Yes. OK. Now, our resources.

Maletesta lowered himself to the damp ground and leaned back against the wall.

Manpower? Hmmm. Well, it's just me. One-armed Gianni, king of the jungle. Their advantage. Equipment? Well, I've got one surprise in my boot. What else? Disciplined? Hell yes, I've gotten this far, haven't I? Well led? Sure. No, you're forgetting something. What is it?

Yes, that's it. The difference in leadership. My advantage. He's crazy. Ergo, a weakness, a flaw in the armor. Boy, you sure need it! Wow, this sure makes me feel better!

Several hours passed and there was a knock at the door. Maletesta was surprised.

A knock? What now, manners?

"Come in," Maletesta answered, playing out the game.

The door opened and an orderly stood in the doorway next to the guard. He was a gray haired man in a carefully kept but worn uniform. His collar and his cuffs were frayed and there were the beginning of raggedy holes in his knees.

"Come," he ordered abruptly.

"Okey-dokey."

Maletesta followed the orderly out and across the square, shadowed by the marching guard behind him.

"Do you speak English?" Maletesta asked.

"Come," the orderly replied.

"Nice night out tonight, isn't it?"

"Come," the orderly repeated.

"Hell," Maletesta uttered and they continued in silence to the main building of the fortress.

TWENTY SEVEN

Borneo

"How do you like being a spy?"

"I'm not a spy and you know it!" Maletesta answered. "The war's over . . . and you know it!"

"The penalty for spying is death."

"Aren't you listening? The war's over! Hirohito surrendered!"

"Spies are a necessary element of warfare, as we all know, but the penalty is always death. A soldier in uniform is protected by the codes of the warrior, but a spy has no such protection."

"Your understanding of the Geneva Convention is impeccable. However, there is no war."

And so the argument had continued for over twenty minutes. John Maletesta, teacher of English literature and former soldier versus Colonel Isuru Tamako, commander in chief of His Imperial Majesty's forces in Borneo, Mount Subu sector. The discussion was carried out in the dining room of Tamako's quarters. Maletesta had been brought there by the orderly and the guard. The guard remained on duty on the other side of the door. The orderly had motioned for Maletesta to sit down in a Windsor chair in one corner of the dining room.

Maletesta sat down, scanning the room. There was a small window, big enough to get through, at the end of the room. He caught a glimpse of interior courtyard beyond. There were two doors in addition to the one he had entered. He did not know here they led. The furnishings in the room were simple, yet an odd mixture of eastern and western decor. There was another Windsor chair near the one in which he was sitting and a small table between them. A single yellow flower from the jungle stood in a black lacquered vase on the table.

In the center of the room was a low dining table where one presumably sat on the floor,

Japanese style, when eating. Along the wall on either side of one of the doors were glass and mahogany exhibit cases, but they were not lighted, so he could not see what was in them.

The cases looked like those he had seen in a college gallery. On the wall above the exhibit cases hung a large rectangular map of the Far East. Maletesta studied it and noticed that the countries controlled by the Japanese in about 1943 were colored red. On the wall opposite was a framed print of the Emperor.

Just when Maletesta was about to get up and walk over to the window, the door near the picture of the Emperor opened and an officer in full ceremonial dress entered.

"I am Colonel Tamako of His Majesty's Imperial Army," he announced in unaccented English and bowed slightly from the waist. He was of medium height, and his head was shaved. A thin whisper of a moustache adorned his upper lip. He wore the katana of the samurai, a sword of rank.

Maletesta stood and returned the bow with a nod of his head.

"John Maletesta of Sister Agatha's College of All Saints, Burlingame, California."

"I do not understand this. Please sit down and explain yourself."

Colonel Tamako took the chair across from the jungle flower and scrutinized Maletesta.

"I teach at a college," Maletesta blurted, the words rushing out without pause. "The college sent two teachers and me on an expedition to search for the origin of man. We had information about fossils in the limestone caves near the volcano. That was our destination. However, we were betrayed and ambushed by our guide, a man named Van Vliet. All of the rest were murdered."

Maletesta inhaled and leaned forward waiting for the response. His eyes were drawn to the sword. The moment in the Philippines flashed though his mind. He flinched.

"Very sad," Colonel Tamako drawled. "The American army is so weak now that it must send one-armed men as spies. Against such a diminished force, victory will soon be ours. My own agent in Sibu has told me that the Americans and the British are in flight throughout the Far East."

"Wait a minute," Maletesta interjected, "wait a minute! What the hell are you talking about?"

The discussion was interrupted by a knock at the door through which Tamako had entered. Tamako said something in Japanese and a servant entered, placed food on the table, and left. Tamako arose from his chair.

"We shall eat now," he said and motioned Maletesta to one side of the low table. He sat on the other side.

Although he was hungry, Maletesta didn't pay attention to what he was eating. He knew it was rice and bamboo shoots and some kind of meat, but his mind was on his predicament. His first strategy had been to reason with the Japanese colonel, assuming that a possible mistake had been made. Van Vliet was a crook, and he was a teacher involved in an expedition seeking knowledge of an ancient evolution. That idea had failed miserably, with Tamako insisting that he was a spy and the war was still on. *What should I try next?*

There was no conversation while they ate. Maletesta labored with his chop sticks. Having only one arm, he could not pick up the rice bowl as was the custom, so he had to lean forward and put his face close to it on the table. Tamako watched him impassively. When they finished, the houseboy appeared and cleared the utensils, leaving just two cups and a pot of tea on the table.

Maletesta breathed deeply. He sipped his tea and then put the cup down on the table.

"How did you learn to speak English so well, Colonel?" he asked.

"I was raised many years ago in Gilroy, California," Tamako replied.

"Gilroy!" Maletesta exclaimed.

Maybe there's an opening here. Old home week or something.

"My father has a friend," Maletesta continued, "who brings him bulbs of fresh garlic from there . . ."

"My father and mother had a farm there," Tamako interrupted. "Your government put them in a concentration camp because they were Japanese. Also my sister and my aunt."

Whoops, not a great opener. To hell with him!

"It wasn't us who pulled the sneak attack on Pearl Harbor!" Maletesta snapped.

"The area is within the co-prosperity sphere of Japan."

"Who decided that? Tojo? Did you ask any of the people you invaded if they wanted to be in the co-prosperity sphere? The people in China, or Burma, or the Philippines? How about the women and children you bayoneted in Nanking? Did you ask them? And the people on Bataan, in the Death March? Did you ask them?"

Maletesta was livid, his eyes blazed. Tamako pursed his lips to control his irritation. He rose and opened a drawer in the closest exhibit case. He extracted a newspaper and turned around. He threw it face up onto the table in front of Maletesta. Maletesta looked at the newspaper which was a tabloid. He did not recognize the language of the headlines and front page articles, but there was no mistaking the central picture of the mushroom cloud. The whole world now recognized the explosion of the atomic bomb in Japan.

"And what of that?" Tamako snarled, pointing at the newspaper. "Were there not thousands of women and children in Hiroshima?"

Maletesta smoothed out the newspaper slowly with his hand. A silence hung in the air between them. Tamako said nothing, his face was still but his fingers were drumming lightly on the table. There was anger in his eyes. A few minutes passed and then Maletesta spoke.

"This proves," Maletesta said, tapping the newspaper with his finger, "that you know the war is over."

"Well done!" Tamako slowly smiled. "Your debating society would be proud of you! You have taken one point and turned it into another! Well done!

"However," he continued, "you do not understand. The war is not 'over.' This phase of the war has ended, but . . ."

"Then," Maletesta interrupted, "what the hell are you doing out here in the jungle? Why don't you let your men go home?"

The colonel laughed.

"My soldiers serve the Emperor. Do you not know the code of Bushido?"

"Bushido?"

"What is your name again?"

"Maletesta."

"Yes. It is so obvious, Maletesta, that you are a young man from a young country. Your understanding of the world is flawed and immature. Ah, well. If the world had given you time, you might have learned of Bushido. Unfortunately, you must die tomorrow. Your death as an American spy is important to my soldiers."

"You know," Maletesta said evenly, "that I'm not a spy and that the war is over. What's the point?"

"The point, as you call it, is destiny: the destiny of the Emperor's co-prosperity and the Japanese people. This war you speak of is merely a stage in the journey. At this time, this stage has not been successful in temporal terms. Now we must rest, prepare and make ready for the next stage. Readiness is all."

"The journey's over," Maletesta snapped. "So is the old regime that ordered it. A new democracy is now being built in Japan."

"Democracy?" Tamako laughed. "I speak of ancient and true things. Democracy, aristocracy...those terms are not relevant. The historic destiny of a people has nothing to do with whatever government is in place."

"People want the freedom to make their own choices. That's what this war was about . . ."

"Freedom? Freedom? Do you mean the freedom my family had in Gilroy? The freedom of the internment camp? Or the freedom to lead a life without purpose? No, Maletesta, what people need is not your simplistic notion of freedom, but to be at one with the truth. That is true freedom."

Tamako was nodding in agreement with himself. Suddenly he asked:

"What did your scientists want?"

"Who?" Maletesta replied .

"The scientists from your expedition. Were they not anthropologists?"

"Until you had them murdered, yes, they were."

"Were they not seeking to be at one with the truth?"

Tamako was now standing, hands on his hips, looking down over the table at the seated Maletesta.

Maletesta stood up.

"This is a game of words, colonel. The fact remains that you had members of a scientific expedition murdered. It was not an act of war; it was an act of dishonor!"

There was a knock at the door before Tamako could respond. He said something and the door opened. A junior officer entered. Maletesta guessed that he was Tamako's adjutant. The adjutant bowed and then gave what appeared to be a brief report. Tamako answered and the adjutant bowed again and left the room.

"I know that you did not come here by yourself," Tamako stated. "I was told that two of the primitive people were with you when my men found you. Now, it appears, there are more out on the perimeter."

Maletesta started, then tried to appear nonchalant.

"I met those two men on the trail. We just all seemed to be going in the same direction, that's all," he explained.

"Ha! Ha! You are a poor liar, Maletesta! Did you live by yourself in the jungle all this time since the ambush? No, of course one of the primitive villages took care of you! And now they are looking for you!"

Maletesta changed his tack. He shrugged his shoulders.

"They mean you no harm," he said. "They're probably a very small group and poorly armed. If your men fire over their heads, they'll run. Leave them alone and they'll go home."

"No harm? No harm? Of course not! They are primitives from this island. They live in the Stone Age! How could they harm us?"

Tamako paused in thinking and then spoke again.

"Sometimes my soldiers hunt them. It is good for training."

"What? Hunt them? What kind of a barbarian are you?" Maletesta shouted.

Tamako had moved over to one of the exhibit cases.

"Barbarian is a flexible word. The British used Maxim machine guns on Africans armed with spears, and yet the teachers in your schools praise the British as a highly 'civilized' society. Your country dropped horrendous bombs on the civilians in our cities. Who are the barbarians?" He waved his right hand in dismissal. "Enough of this barbarian talk."

Tamako pressed a light switch near the cases.

Both cases lit up, revealing the contents within. Maletesta looked into the cases. He walked around the table for a closer look. Inside the cases he saw dozens of fossilized bones, some of them tagged with small tags bearing apparent descriptions in Chinese. Larger pieces were accompanied by 3X5 cards. There was a large white card at the end of the case typed in English, *PEKING MAN.*

Maletesta gasped.

"My God, it's Peking Man!" he exclaimed. "It's Peking Man!"

"You know it, then?" Tamako asked.

"She was right," Maletesta mumbled, almost to himself. "A wild story, a long shot, and here it is. Holy Cow. Peking Man." He paced along the cases, peering into their interior at the bones. The artifacts were carefully arranged in the cases, showing the hand of someone who knew exhibits.

"I can guess," Maletesta said, looking over at Tamako, "that you're an anthropologist, too. In addition to being a murderer and a thief, of course."

"Thief, Maletesta? How am I a thief?" A puzzled expression appeared on Tamako's face.

"Now you're going to tell me that the Chinese gave these to you?" Maletesta countered. "As a gesture of their gratitude for being invaded?"

"You are too stupid, Maletesta! Too stupid!"

Tamako began to strut in his anger. He began to splutter.

"This discovery belongs to the co-prosperity sphere! It does not belong to the Americans!

Or the French! Or the English! It belongs to the Asian!"

"It belongs to the world!" Maletesta said. "It doesn't belong to any particular race."

"Ha!' Tamako replied, "and who do these belong to?"

At the end of the exhibit case nearest the hallway door, there was a mound of small pouches in the corner next to what appeared to be several jaw fragments.

Tamako lifted the glass door in the top of the case and brought out one of the pouches.

Maletesta recognized it as very similar to the pouch found on Talah. He awaited Tamako's next move.

"Look," Tamako said quietly.

He turned to the table and poured out the contents. A shower of precious stones cascaded down on the table top. He laughed gleefully.

"Who to these belong to?" he asked Maletesta.

"I don't know. Where did you steal them?"

Tamako was angry at the accusation.

"They were being smuggled from Asia to America in the crates," he said smugly. "Tell me, Maletesta, who do they belong to? You have no quick answer? I'll tell you. They belong to the soldiers of the Emperor, waiting and preparing for the next stage of the co-prosperity sphere!"

"The Emperor has been deposed," Maletesta stated.

Maletesta was beginning to feel depressed. For some inexplicable reason, his left arm hurt. He massaged his shoulder with his right hand.

To have come so far and now no farther...Peking Man...Sister Agatha's long shot... Robidoux...Le Boo.

Bones and jewels. Talah's father must have been one of the workers who moved the crates upriver from Sibu. The caves.

Gone. So close and now buried in this mountain. Everything slipping away...slipping away in the blind power of this madman. Gianni, think of something! Try something. One more try.

"Colonel," he said, "our countries are working together now..."

"No! Never!" Tamako interjected.

"Together," Maletesta resumed, looking for the right words. "Like when you were growing up with your family, in school..."

"Ha! In school? 'Don't let that Jap in here!' Together? 'Can the Jap talk?' Together? No, Maletesta, not together. 'No Japs allowed!' Never! Not even to play American Legion baseball. 'No Japs allowed!' No, Maletesta, never together!"

"You played baseball?" Maletesta asked incredulously.

"Yes."

"What position?"

"Third base. Not on a team."

Tamako lowered his voice.

"In the yard behind my father's house."

Tamako held an imaginary bat in his hands and swung.

"I could hit too. I hit rocks all day. At one time my father was...enough! You must return to your cell now!"

Tamako walked over and pulled a bell pull next to the door. There was a knock at the door and then the orderly appeared, received his command and left.

"Too bad," Maletesta said. "I played baseball too."

"Where?"

"Where ever I could. In the street. In the playground, in high school, college..."

"Can you pitch?" Tamako asked anxiously.

"Well, I was actually a centerfielder..."

"Can you pitch?" Tamako insisted.

He watched Maletesta intently.

"I pitched once or twice at Funston, pickup games, whoever showed up, played..."

There was another knock at the door and this time the orderly entered with two guards.

They advanced toward Maletesta, but at a command from Tamako, they stopped and stood at attention. Tamako frowned for a moment and then walked to within a foot of Maletesta and looked into his face. Maletesta could see a strange glint in his eyes.

"Some Americans like to gamble," Tamako said slowly, "Do you like to gamble?"

"Sure, what's the bet?"

"Maletesta, it is a very large bet," Tamako roared, immensely pleased with himself.

"It is your life!"

"What? What do you mean?" Maletesta involuntarily stepped back.

"Tomorrow. In the courtyard. You will try to strike me out. If you do, I will let you live. If you do not, I will kill you myself."

Tamako's hand tightened again on the sword. Before Maletesta could answer, he barked another command and the guards grabbed Maletesta and marched him out of the room.

After they left, Tamako returned to one of the exhibit cases and, bending down, pulled out one of the drawers at the bottom. It held a baseball bat, very old and dented, but without cracks or chips. He held it in his hands lovingly. Then he stood up and assumed the batter's stance. He watched the imaginary ball approach and swung. He coiled back and swung again.

TWENTY EIGHT

Borneo

It was the same dream again. Japanese soldiers were chasing him. His feet felt like they were in mud. He was too slow. He saw them approaching. They had baseball bats in their hands.

God!

He woke up and laughed in spite of himself.

God! Now they've got the bats! I'm losing my mind. This can't be true. If I strike out this crazy colonel, I'll live?

It was as crazy as the whole expedition. He never really expected to find the missing crates of Peking Man. And there they were, up in Tamako's dining room.

Who would believe it? Who could believe any of this crazy setup? A secret base hidden in the jungle, waiting for what? Better believe it, Gianni boy, because it's all true, including your debut on the mound tomorrow morning. When was the last time you pitched?

He started pacing again, trying to remember.

It was at Funston, I know that for sure. One of those pickup games I played on the weekends in high school. Six years ago? Yeah. Funston, what a park, even DiMaggio had played there at one time. OK, enough of the history lesson. How is the arm?

He spent a lot of time in the hospital getting his right arm back to strength during recovery, working with a barbell. Once, after being released, he drove down the coast to Pescadero and walked along the beach. He picked up the little blue rocks with the holes in them and flung them into the surf. He made a mental note to find out how the rocks got holes in them, but never did find out. Now, in his cell, he knew his arm was strong and the work in the village had made it stronger.

But can I pitch?

He got down on his knees and scrambled around the cell in the dark, feeling the ground for something to throw.

In a few minutes he assembled a collection of small rocks and rotting pieces of wood.

He piled his practice balls near the door and paced off the distance to the opposite wall. At a distance about waist-high from the floor, he scratched a line into the wall with one of the rocks. Then he retreated back to his pile near the door.

Why am I scratching a mark in a wall I can't see? I don't know. It's the only drill I know. Throw at a target. There's no other choice.

He picked up a rock. He tried to remember the motion.

Face the batter. No, that won't work. Pitch from the stretch. OK. Bring with your hands together. That's a big help, only one hand! Bring your left leg up and back. Flamingo. Yeah. I remember now. Lift. Ha, I can do it! Bring the arm back. Uh oh. Can't keep my balance. Scrap that position. Leave the left foot on the ground. Bring the arm back. Throw. Release. Follow through. Back foot comes forward.

The rock smacked on the wall.

Where did it hit? It doesn't matter. Pick up another one. Smack. A piece of wood. Thud. More rocks. God! What was that? He shook his hand. Some kind of worm had crawled into the pile.

Throw a curve, Gianni. Can you remember? Always threw too many fastballs. Once they started to hit them, somebody else came into pitch. Let's see, how did I throw that curve? This is stupid! You can't throw a curve with a rock! The hell with it. What time is it? How much time before my execution? Mother of God, what a mess.

He sat down on his pile of straw and tried to remember the pitchers he had seen. *Seals Stadium.* He could see the batting practice before the game with his father and him standing behind the home dugout. "Red hot! Get your Red hot here! Red hot!" An ambitious hot dog vendor threaded his way through the near empty pre-game stands. The ground crew was chalking lines, raking the pitcher's mound. The smell of the freshly cut grass and the sounds of the players calling to each other while they worked out. Down in the bullpen the pitcher was warming up. There was an easiness to it, a grace beyond description. Even when the hated Oaks were in town, his excitement surpassed his animosity toward the cross Bay rivals. They were all *baseball* players, friend and foe alike.

"Watch that pitcher, Gianni," Pop would say in that soft spoken way of his. "He throws like Lefty Grove. See? Smooth. Batter can't pick up the ball til it's too late. He keeps pitching like that, he'll be in the majors soon."

Pop. Mama. If only I could get word to them somehow that I'm OK. OK? Wake up, Maletesta! You're OK? Tomorrow, a crazy colonel's going to cut your head off with his damned sword!

He knelt down on the floor and began retrieving the rocks.

The guard outside listened to the sound of the rocks hitting against the wall. He was anxious about it, but, after circling the cellblock building and seeing no damage to the walls, he relaxed. The sound irritated him, but he assumed the American spy had gone crazy. He was relieved when the sound stopped a half-hour later and it was quiet inside the cell.

TWENTY NINE

Borneo

Hulang was grinning from ear to ear, as he crouched in the underbrush watching two Japanese soldiers firing at where he was a few minutes ago. He could see them through a small opening in the vines which surrounded him. They were speaking quietly to each other even as they fired. He knew they were angry and confused at the ineffectiveness of their rifle fire. Eventually, after much noise with their rifles, they stopped.

The brush was too dense for any easy movement forward. The soldiers attempted it, and then gave up. Reluctantly, they began to backtrack to their company. As they turned, one of them suddenly grabbed at his neck. He started shaking violently. He dropped his rifle and waved his arms, stumbling toward his partner. Then he fell to the jungle floor, dead. The aim of one of the villager's blowpipes had been true. The other soldier was now screaming. He ran in the direction of his company, pausing every few minutes to turn and fire his rifle wildly. Soon he disappeared from Hulang's view and hearing.

It was the way the morning had gone. The Japanese had been overconfident. In the past, it had been easy sport to snipe at the Borneo people with their telescoped rifles. The local people were unaware of the one to two hundred yard range of the rifles. Soon, though, they learned to give the base a wide berth. It was the bad luck of Maletesta's party that they were spotted by a Japanese patrol that had ranged farther than usual from the fort.

However, this time Colonel Tamako had ordered a company to pursue the villagers into the bush. He did not like the idea of their alliance with strangers like Maletesta and decided to teach them a lesson. There was no telling what would happen if the they lost their fear of the Japanese. So Captain Ihiru, the adjutant, took his men out at first light to pursue and destroy the bothersome interlopers.

Ihiru and his soldiers were rusty. They had not fought an action in almost two years, but they were convinced of their invincibility. Therefore, they made mistakes. They sighted Hulang's party about a half mile from the base. It appeared that Hulang was leading his people up the trail back into the deep woods adjoining the jungle. Ihiru split his command and ordered a double time march after them. He took half the company to the right, and his sergeant took the other half to the left. The intention was to join in a pincer movement on Hulang's group.

As soon as Hulang's war party was out of sight of the Japanese, they abandoned the trail and moved perpendicularly from it quickly through the bush. They were masters at moving quickly and silently in this environment. It was mother and father to them. The spirits of the trees, and plants, and rocks were their spirits. They were as one with them. In a very short time, they were poised to attack the right half of the company.

Hulang and his hunters did not make war like a 20th Century military apparatus. They attacked by hitting one soldier with a blowpipe dart. Then they withdrew. The fatal wound was delivered silently. Therefore, the soldiers had no idea of the direction from which it came. They fired wildly, but Hulang's men were gone by then. It was like a game for them. A soldier would feel a tug at his foot.

The soldier looked down. There was nothing there. Maybe it was a root. He thought he heard something. An animal? He hesitated. He wasn't as close to his comrades as he was a few minutes earlier. The sudden blow of a parang was swift and deadly. A muted gurgle was his last sound. When the soldiers reunited in the next clearing, one would be missing.

As the hours passed, the soldiers became more fearful and more frustrated. There were no enemy targets. There were no enemy casualties.

At 9:30, Captain Ihiru called the action off. He had lost five men and morale was sinking rapidly. He withdrew his contingent of the company and gave the pre-arranged signal for the other half of the company to withdraw. The company reformed at a clearing about a quarter of a quarter mile from the base. Three men from the other contingent were killed or missing. The sergeant thought that some of Hulang's men had been hit by rifle fire, but there were no confirmed kills. Ihiru commended the men on their courage, and then they assembled in formation and marched sullenly back to the base.

Hulang watched the soldiers leave from a vantage point half way up a tree. He gave permission to his hunters to begin the ritual removal of the enemies' heads. They also salvaged whatever items may be of use to the village: knives, tobacco, knapsacks--coins and charms for decoration. They didn't take rifles or uniforms. Some helmets were taken because they made excellent pots.

Hulang had ordered Talah to stay in the same tree when the soldiers were coming. She had scampered down after they retreated, but he did not know where she was now. He climbed down from the tree and brought his hunting party together. They would eat and then smoke and then rest. Then he would decide their next move.

THIRTY

Borneo

Colonel Tamako was a life-long early riser. Very few of his soldiers knew that he was a Buddhist and meditated each morning before the sun arose. Then he completed a series of physical exercises. This morning was special to Tamako. When he finished his early morning routine, he left his bedroom and walked to the dining room. It was still dark outside but he did not need any lights. He opened the lower drawer of the exhibit case where the baseball bat had lain and extracted a package from under a layer of rattan. He carried the package back into his bedroom.

He laid the package down on a mat and stared at it momentarily. The package was double wrapped in oilskins and a water proof parachute material. He touched the wrappings lightly, and then he carefully removed the outer and inner layers. He unfolded the uniform the package had contained. He smiled as he beheld it.

He smoothed out the wrinkles with his hands and caressed the letters. It smelled a little moldy, but was still in excellent condition. The cap was more distressed but serviceable. He worried about the shoes. They were cracked and verdigris encrusted the brass eyelets. He scraped the shoes lovingly with a brush. They would do fine.

Colonel Tamako's thoughts went to a summer long ago. He was twenty three years old, working on the farm. His father had saved enough money from several years of his artichoke harvests to send young Isuru and his sister to stay in Tokyo with their grandparents for a month.

It had been a vivid and startling experience for him. Young Isuru felt reunited with something from which he'd been separated. He was at one with the people around him. They were his people. Nobody stared at him; nobody moved away from him. He was no longer the outsider. He was not *Nisei*, he was *Japanese*.

One night near the end of his holiday, his grandfather came home and told Isuru that he had a special surprise for him. A very special event would take place in two days. His grandfather could barely contain himself with his elation, but he would not tell Isuru about the event.

"You must wait," was all that his grandfather said.

Early in the morning two days later, Isuru and his grandfather boarded a tram and rode for almost an hour through Tokyo and the outlying districts. When they reached their destination, his grandfather extracted two tickets from his wallet and showed them to Isuru. The boy looked at them but could not believe what he read.

"It can't be," he said.

His grandfather's eyes twinkled.

"It is," he said.

Colonel Tamako was dressed now. He folded the wrappings and placed them in a corner. Then he summoned his orderly.

THIRTY ONE

Borneo

Maletesta felt something kicking at the bottom of his foot. A guttural voice was saying something but he couldn't understand.

Leave me alone. Let me sleep.

There was a harder kick and he awoke. The door to the cell was open and two guards were standing over him. He squeezed his eyes shut in the morning light and opened them again. They were still there, motioning him to get up. One of them made a move to prod him with his bayonet. Maletesta jumped up and backed away from the guard.

Should I take him now?

The butterfly knife from Munoz was inside his shirt. Easy reach. During the night he moved it from his boot, where he had kept it since he left San Francisco.

I can probably kill the two of them if I move quick enough. Why? I'd never get across the compound. The two guards have rifles. Better wait. Play out this hand.

They pushed him through the cell door and out into the sun. As they marched across the compound, he glanced at the crew who were adding the finishing touches to the gallows. They were hammering in the early morning heat. Sweat glistened off their bodies.

This Tamako is crazy: he's going to hang me and kill me with his sword. Can't make up his mind I guess.

His arm felt good. After his late night practice, he had slept soundly. He thought he should sing, but he couldn't think of an appropriate song.

A religious song? High Mass? The Gloria? "Patrem omni potentem . . ." No. Need something with a little more punch. What?

Then he remembered a song he sang in the eighth grade play. "Joshua Fit the Battle of Jericho." They were all dressed in bed sheets their mothers had hemmed into some kind of Middle Eastern-looking costume. Beards were applied with burnt cork.

"Joshua fit the battle of Jericho," Maletesta began singing as he marched along, "Jericho, Jericho. Joshua fit the battle of Jericho, and the walls come tumbling down."

The guards looked at him and winced. Oddly enough, he could whistle on key, but his singing voice had a mind of its own. He didn't care. He started another chorus. As he was singing, Captain Ihiru and his company came back into the base. Maletesta stopped to look at them while they entered. He guessed that they were the company sent "to hunt the 'primitives,'" and, from the looks on their faces, the "hunting" had not gone well. Captain Ihiru left his men and joined Maletesta and the two guards at the foot of the stairs which led to the Colonel's quarters.

"Well, tallyho and all that! Hunting wasn't so good, huh? No easy targets today? No sitting ducks?"

Maletesta smiled at Ihiru who did not understand him, but recognized a jeer in any language. He spat at Maletesta's feet and started up the stairs. The guards and Maletesta followed.

"A hunting we will go, a hunting we will go," Maletesta sang as he marched up the stairs. He could feel the knife bouncing inside his shirt as he landed on each tread.

When? Wait.

Finally the four of them, after knocking on the door and being told to enter, were back in the room with the exhibit cases.

Maletesta's jaw almost dropped. Colonel Tamako stood on the other side of the table . . . in a complete Chicago White Sox uniform! The only non-regulation item was the ever-present sword of the samurai, the katana. Tamako smiled and bowed to Maletesta.

"You are shocked, I can see," he said.

"Where the hell did you get that?" Maletesta asked incredulously. He had only seen them in magazines.

"Fifteen years ago, I played baseball in Tokyo with major leaguers." Tamako picked up the bat and swung it viciously. "You ever play with major leaguers, Maletesta?"

"Major league baseball? In Japan?" Maletesta was at a loss.

"Lefty O'Doul, Ted Lyons, Moe Berg, others who loved baseball."

"Lefty O'Doul!"

I have lost my mind. Peking Man, a White Sox uniform and someone who played with Lefty O'Doul here in the middle of Borneo. Nobody would ever believe it.

Tamako sighed. On second glance, Maletesta noticed that the uniform was badly faded and smelled moldy.

"And now, play ball!" he announced and walked around the table and out through the door which his orderly had entered the night before.

Maletesta looked at Captain Ihiru and his guards. They tried to conceal the surprised looks on their faces and quickly returned to military bearing. Ihiru motioned to Maletesta to follow Tamako and they fell in rank behind him. There was a small kitchen on the other side of the door and then a door leading outside to a stairway down to a small courtyard framed by two other buildings and an interior wall. As Maletesta descended the stairs, he saw Tamako at the bottom. Tamako stopped about thirty feet away from the stairs and began to draw on side of the building with a chunk of charcoal.

They marched Maletesta to a stake in the ground half way across the courtyard.

"Pitcher's mound, I suppose," Maletesta noted, as the guards left him there and exited through a door in the wall which presumably led to the compound. Ihiru walked over to Tamako and stood at attention. Maletesta watched Tamako curiously.

"Strike zone!" Tamako barked, as if he could read Maletesta's mind. He had completed a rectangle that roughly outlined the area between his knees and his shoulders lengthwise and was about two feet wide. Then he lined himself up like a batter in front of it. He was obviously pleased with himself and laughed.

"See, Maletesta, Captain Ihiru is now the umpire! He can see where the ball will hit.

Nothing will be left to guessing!"

With that, Tamako said something to Ihiru and the captain moved closer to the building and stood at ease. Tamako then picked up a baseball bat which was leaning against the wall. He took some practice swings and then stood in front of his hand drawn strike zone.

"Batter up!" he shouted gleefully and took another huge cut with the bat.

This has to be a nightmare.

Maletesta looked at the scene in front of him: to his left, Ihiru, holding a baseball, looking a bit confused and then Tamako at the "plate."

What pitcher ever faced a batter who wore a sword? And was going to use it on you if you didn't get him out! The sports guys on the radio used to talk about sudden death. They didn't mean this.

Tamako and Ihiru both stood in the shadow provided by the balcony overhead. The late morning sun was on the pitcher.

Good. Maybe the ball coming out of the light will be harder to see.

"Batter up!" Tamako shouted again.

Ihiru rolled the ball out to Maletesta underhand.

Maletesta stooped and picked it up. It was old and also felt moldy, but it also felt good in his hand. It was the first baseball he'd picked up since that fateful night in the Philippines. His fingers squeezed it and he paced back a few steps from the stake in the ground. He rolled the the ball in his hand, stopping with two fingers across the seams.

He returned to the stake, looked down at Tamako, reared back and threw quickly.

The ball smacked against the wall inside the chalk marks.

"Stri!" Ihiru announced.

Tamako leaned the bat against his leg and spat on his hands.

"Very quick, but now I'm ready," he called to Maletesta.

"Yeah, like you weren't before," Maletesta mumbled and again threw quickly.

"Bah," Ihiru shouted, approximating the sound for "ball." Then he picked the ball up and rolled it back to the pitcher.

Bah, indeed! Damn!

"Hey, pitcher! You got anything? Down the middle!" Tamako jeered, taking another swing.

He swings well, but he doesn't keep his head down. What does that tell me? That he can't hit a curve? Maybe. Can I throw one?

He drew his arm back again.

Mechanics. How? I can't even keep balanced! Throw with the snap. Throw!

The ball thudded against the wall again. Tamako did not swing at it.

"Bah!"

"Down the middle, pitcher! Down the middle!" the batter shouted.

"Screw you!"

All right, Gianni, all right. Try it again. Look at him. He let the high ones go by. I bet he can't see the low ones. Over confident. Why not? He's got the sword. And Ihiru. And his soldiers. Concentrate, damn it! Arm back. Elbow as high as your shoulder. Ball to the wall. Fire!

Tamako took a mighty swing and missed as the ball went by him and thudded into the wall.

"Stri!" Ihiru announced again, looking at where the ball had hit the wall.

Tamako glared at him as he straightened up and took a few cuts.

"Right down the middle, batter! Can't you hit it?" Maletesta laughed and called in from his mound, the stake.

Tamako spat on the ground.

"Lucky pitch for one-arm! Ha. Ha. Ha!" he said and took another swing.

Maletesta picked up the ball again.

"Two and two, chump! Two and two."

Maletesta set the ball on the ground to wipe his eyes with his sleeve. Sweat was pouring down his face and his shirt was blotched with it. The heat of the day was beginning to rise in the little courtyard. He wiped his hand on his pants and stooped to pick up the ball. There was a small rock near it on the ground and he picked it up with the ball.

Scuff it! Scuff it!

He held the ball behind his back and looked in at the batter. Tamako stood ready at the plate, swinging slowly and shifting his feet. His eyes glared out at Maletesta from under the White Sox cap. The katana moved with the swing, creating the illusion of a straight line from end of bat to tip of sword. Ihiru stood impassively, one hand resting on his belt holster and the other in his pocket.

Scuff it!

Maletesta pressed the rock into the ball behind his back. His thumb hurt as he rolled it back and forth over the rock.

Is it cutting enough to affect the flight? I can't tell. Hell, I've never done it before, only heard about it. How much was enough?

"Hey, pitcher, throw the ball! The fans are getting impatient! Too slow! Ha. Ha. Ha." Tamako shook his bat at Maletesta.

Maletesta let the rock drop and gripped the ball with his thumb on the back seam and the upper seam between his index and middle seam. His fingers ached. He realized that he was holding the ball in a death grip and released some of the pressure.

That's better. Easy now. Relax.

He looked in at Tamako, putting on his best opposing pitcher's face. Tamako stood there, rocking on his heels, a smirk on his face, the bat held easily.

Maletesta went into his stretch. He drew his arm back, saw his imaginary target and threw. He watched the scuffed ball move strangely at the end of its flight. It sailed near the strike zone, but not near enough. It thudded against the building: high and outside.

"Bah," Ihiru grunted, stooping to pick the ball up off the ground. He rolled it underhanded back toward Maletesta.

Christ! Is this real? Another ball and this bastard'll be after me with his sword? The butterfly knife. Against the sword? Good luck! They wouldn't have let me go anyway. Well, throw it and go for it. If I could get the adjutant, grab his pistol...and what will Tamako be doing all that time? Can I pray? Who was that Italian saint Mama liked? Italians need to stick together here. Mother Cabrini. Yeah, stick together here. Gianni! You're going crazy: throw the ball and get it over with!

Maletesta picked up the ball and rotated it in his hand, looking for the seams he wanted. He heard Tamako say something in Japanese, but he wasn't paying attention. He looked up and he saw the stands in Seals Stadium. The owner of the Seals was sitting in the lower boxes, watching him. He was wearing a straw boater and was leaning forward, hands on his knees. Two men sat next to him, one holding a clip board.

The owner was nodding at *him*, John Maletesta. The batting coach near the dugout called out something to the pitcher on the mound. The pitcher had a bucket of balls at his feet. No one else was in the stadium except some seagulls making a racket out in the bleachers, fighting over yesterday's crumbs. He felt good at the plate. Cocky. He was ready. The first pitch came in. He connected...

He released the fast ball.

Tamako corkscrewed over the inside pitch.

The ball thudded against the wall and rolled to the adjutant's feet.

Strike three, the umpire said. Mighty Casey has struck out! Strike three!

Maletesta couldn't contain his elation.

"You're outta here!" he shouted at the batter.

Tamako glared at him and cursed. Then he threw the bat to the side. Then he put his hand on the hilt of the katana. Maletesta felt his blood drain to his feet. His intestines tightened.

He was going to be sick. The ground was moving. A ripple in the ground. He staggered to regain his balance.

I'm not sick! It's real! The ground is moving!

The ripple moved along the ground toward Tamako and Ihiru. Another ripple followed it. They stood stunned and transfixed by the movement, Tamako with the katana drawn partially out of the metal scabbard. The ripple was under them and then into the building. There was a simultaneous rumbling from the bowels of the earth.

Earthquake!

A series of spider web-like cracks suddenly appeared on the side of the building. There was a creaking sound and some loud pops.

Maletesta sensed what was happening around him but was not yet aware. He was a spectator, like the other two people in the courtyard, unable to move. Tamako, frozen with his sword in his hand, mouthed a scream as the balcony crumbled down on him, half burying him in rubble. The falling balcony missed Ihiru, but he cried out and then realized that his commander was dead. He paused, looking blankly at Tamako's body and then he remembered Maletesta. He reached to undo the flap of his holster as he turned toward the mound. His eyes opened wide as Maletesta descended upon him, butterfly knife in hand. He scrabbled frantically at the Nambu pistol in his holster, but Maletesta's knife was quicker. He fell dying beside his commander in the courtyard.

Maletesta could hear the soldiers yelling and engines revving. They were abandoning the danger of the crumbling fort for the jungle. The first tremble of the quake was over, but he knew there would be aftershocks. How many times had he heard the stories about the '06 quake and the aftershocks?

The stairs back up into the building were still intact though the frame was pulled slightly away from the wall.

Why?

The balcony had come down. It didn't make sense to him, the vagaries of an earthquake. He tested the first step with his foot. It held him. He took another step.

Don't waste time!

He bolted up the stairs and they wobbled beneath him.

Once inside the building, he made his way to Tamako's quarters. Everything was a shambles in the kitchen and the hallways with food, furniture, and utensils thrown everywhere.

Great gaps had appeared in the walls, and door jambs were askew. He pushed aside a chair which had fallen across the doorway to Tamako's dining room. The room was a mess. One of the exhibit cases had pitched forward and crashed on the table, spilling bones, tags and 3X5 cards all over the floor. The other one was splintered but still standing. He moved quickly to it, not knowing how much time he had.

The glass was broken and the artifacts and 3X5 cards of Peking Man were jumbled throughout the case. He reached into the case and picked up a jawbone with a few teeth in it. He shoved it and some smaller bones inside his shirt. He tried to make sense of the identification tags but they were written in Chinese.

Which one for which bone?

There was a shiver of movement in the floor.

No time! Get out!

When Maletesta turned he saw the pouches of precious stones lying in the splintered case. Suddenly a shudder ran slowly through the building and the floor shifted even more. He smelled smoke from somewhere below.

Get the hell out, you idiot! After shocks!

He grabbed two of the pouches and shoved them into his shirt with the bones. Then he headed for the door--stepping on the picture of the Emperor as he left.

Maletesta was barely off the last stair outside when the first aftershock hit. He staggered to the middle of the courtyard to avoid falling debris. He looked back and saw Tamako's dream in its death throes. One of the courtyard walls was down now. Fires had broken out in other buildings.

As he ran across the compound, he saw that his former cell had collapsed and the gallows now stood unattended. There were no soldiers to be seen.

Where are the soldiers? Gone. Where? Move quickly, but be careful.

Another rumble from the ground. One of the wall trees went down with a section of the wall. The main gate was shattered. He rushed through it and into the first cover he could find. He crouched and ran through the brush back toward where he was captured. He did not see any soldiers.

Can I find my way back to the village? Without directions or a weapon?

A half hour later, he stopped to rest. He was near the grove of trees where they rested before walking into the sniper fire. The ground had been rising steadily all the way from the fort and he was now out of breath. He found a niche in some rocks which he could lie in and be sheltered from the sight of the casual passerby. He slipped in gratefully and looked back Tamako's fortress.

The sky had darkened and there were smells he could not identify as he scrambled through the brush. Now he knew. Mount Subu was no longer an inactive volcano. He saw the smoke and watched the flow of rocks, debris, mud, and lava which would eventually cover the Japanese base.

And Peking Man. There would be nothing left.

Just like it was a dream. No, a nightmare.

He sighed and arose to continue his journey. He must find another safe place before nightfall. Just inside the grove, he heard a rustle in the brush nearby. He dove behind the largest tree and flung himself to the ground.

No! No! Not again. No!

He clung to the dirt as if it were a shield.

I can't fight anymore! God let me die quickly. I can't take any more!

He squeezed his eyes shut as hard as he could, like a child shutting out the world.

"John, Cowboy John! Oh good! John! It's OK!"

Maletesta opened his eyes. He saw Talah, a huge smile on her face. He rose to his knees and she threw herself at him. He could say nothing, but hugged her with his arm. Tears poured down both of their cheeks.

Behind Talah, Hulang stood with four of his hunters. Hulang also had a smile, gaps between his teeth and all. One of the hunters held up a string of heads which were dangling by his side. One of the heads was from a Japanese soldier. The other two were Van Vliet and Kwan.

THIRTY-TWO

Burlingame, California

Sister Agatha was in her room packing a small suitcase. Her personal belongs were meager. *An Imitation of Christ* by Thomas a Kempis, some scarves and mittens, her rimless spectacles, two tooth brushes, a tube of tooth paste, and family photographs. Her magnificent globe was already boxed in her old office. Today was her last day at All Saints. She had been reassigned to Sacred Heart Grammar School in Vallejo. She whispered the old song again as she packed, though it held no pleasure for her now.

"I heard a blind piper
Playing ninety-five hundred fine songs
And a goat standing by
Playing Mattie Malone on the tongs."

The new President had been in office for a week now. She was from Santa Barbara. Very cordial. Very correct. Very well-mannered. A memorandum had been sent to all of the teachers requesting a description of their political and religious beliefs and their qualifications for the subject they taught. There were already some disgruntled responses from a few teachers to Sister Agatha, but there was nothing she could do about it. She knew All Saints would not be the same.

Sister Agatha shook her head as she snapped the latches of her old suitcase closed. The lines under her eyes and around her mouth had deepened over the past three months. She walked slowly and kept her eyes averted from her acquaintances. Not an hour went by when the expedition and the loss of all those lives didn't enter her mind. *My fault: all my fault.*

There was a knock at the door.

"Come in," she said.

A young nun entered the room, a look of concern on her face. She was new to the school, a novice who would work as a teaching assistant in the Fall semester which began in another week. She had heard the stories about Sister Agatha and consequently, she was a little afraid of her. She stood in the doorway and didn't say anything.

"Well, what is it?" Sister Agatha asked. "Don't just stand there. What is it?"

"Good morning, Sister. You…you have two visitors," the other nun stammered.

"Visitors? Who? My brother's not due until four."

"I don't know, Sister. Sister Clare told me to tell you they were in the visitor's room."

"All right. Thank you."

The young novice exited and Sister Agatha followed a few minutes later. It wouldn't be Uncle Con, she thought, he had visited last week. She crossed the commons under a heavy sky of impending September rain. Maletesta's dog, Carmen, was no longer on campus. She had been given to his parents when Sister Agatha's reassignment came. Dogs were no longer allowed on the campus of All Saints.

There wasn't much activity on campus on this Sunday afternoon. Students2 wouldn't arrive for registration and dormitory assignment until the following Thursday. She entered the main building and nodded to the nun at the reception desk. Her face was white.

"What's the matter, Sister?" Sister Agatha queried, and then she remembered that she was no longer President and her times of concern about the staff were over. She could no longer order the receptionist to the sick bay, or request that she stick out her tongue. It didn't matter anyway. The nun at the desk merely motioned Sister Agatha toward the visitor's room.

"Take a long walk around the commons on your break," Sister Agatha advised, "you need some air in you."

She pulled back the heavy door which led into the visitors' room and walked through.

"Mother of God!"

She thought she would fall, and the room was spinning in front of her. She grabbed at the nearest high-backed chair to steady herself, gripping the hardwood arm with all of her might. Her heart pounded inside her chest. *Mother of God! It can't be! No! Yes! I don't understand. I adore thee oh Christ and I bless thee because by...*

Sitting at the visitor's table was John Maletesta. A pretty little dark-haired girl was sitting next to him. Maletesta stood up, a big grin on his face, and placed a jawbone on the table.

"Peking Man, Sister. But I can't prove it," he announced.

For the first time in her life, the nun was at a loss for words, speechless.

"And these little beauties," Maletesta laughed, laying a half dozen precious gems next to the jawbone, "are for All Saints...but only if you are the president."

9 781647 191351